Who Killed Billy Roller?

The Rhonda Pohs Mysteries Book Six

Sherry Derr-Wille

Published by Rogue Phoenix Press, LLP
Copyright © 2025

ISBN: 978-1-62420-845-4

Credits
Cover Artist: Designs by Ms G
Editor: Amanda Armstrong

Dedication

To everyone who's waiting for this last book of the series.

Chapter One

Are you ready for our night of chaperoning the kids?" Mark asked as they prepared to leave to pick up Jennifer and her new boyfriend, Paul.

"As ready as I'll ever be. I'm looking forward to seeing Bill and the members of his band. I remember when you first started coaching at the high school. I knew they were destined for great things even before they won that talent show in Chicago."

Rhonda dropped her detective's shield into her purse. If the kids got too rowdy, she could flash it and remind them she was a police officer and, even off duty, could easily arrest the troublemakers.

Jen and Paul were waiting for them when they pulled up to the apartment house where they'd moved just weeks earlier.

"I can't believe you were able to get us approved to be chaperones," Jen said as soon as they got into the car.

"It wasn't hard. There weren't many of the teachers who wanted the job. I figured it would be safe enough with two of Clark County's finest along with me. I did take a lot of flak from the kids, but that's part of being a member of the faculty. You know how kids are about the older generation horning in on their get-togethers. I had to remind them with the show being held on school property, having chaperones was a must."

Paul laughed.

"I can understand these kids. Back in the day, I certainly didn't want adults putting a damper on the things I liked to do with my friends."

"I can only imagine what you were doing," Jen teased.

"It's not as bad as you think. I wasn't drinking or having sex. When I was in high school, I spent a lot of time learning how to play poker online. I never lost money or anything like that, but I did learn how to play the games.

Being a computer geek helped me in learning how to beat the house on the slots and I've always been good at Blackjack."

"Sounds harmless enough," Mark mused.

"It was until I got to college and started playing for money with my fraternity brothers. I took them for quite a bit until their fathers complained and it got back to my old man. Of course, by that time, I was twenty-one and started investing my winnings at the casinos here in town. The rest, as they say, is history."

"It sounds like you're good at what you do, otherwise, you and Jen couldn't afford that fancy new apartment of yours," Rhonda commented.

"He is," Jen replied. "Thanks to your friend Tyson, that's how he got his job. He's not at the top of the ladder like Tyson is, but he's got his foot in the door and the money is good. I'm sure he will go far with that company."

Rhonda smiled. She knew Paul worked for the same company as Tyson. It didn't come as a surprise their friend connected him with the owners of the company along with a good recommendation.

~ * ~

Even though they'd arrived early for the performance, the auditorium was filled with teenagers, all talking at once about the upcoming show.

"How do you put up with this every day?" Jen asked.

Mark laughed at her comment. "I might ask you the same thing. How do you put up with murders daily? To answer your question, though, they aren't always this hyped up. Admit it, you're as pumped as the kids about the show. Once they start to play, these kids will calm down a bit."

They were about to take their seats, when Billy's manager, Rusty Phillips came up to Mark. "Mr. Pohs, it's good to see you again. You too, Mrs. Phos. I was wondering if the two of you could come backstage with me."

Rhonda and Mark exchanged anxious glances. Something was wrong. They knew Rusty as well as they did Bill, and something was off about the demeanor of the young man.

"You two get all the luck," Jen said pretending to pout. "I'd give anything to meet Billy Roller."

Rusty looked at Jen skeptically. "And you are?"

"I'm sorry, I should have made introductions before this," Rhonda apologized. This is my partner at the Sheriff's Office, Jen Sims. Do you think Bill would mind if she came along with us?"

"It might be a good idea, Mrs. Pohs."

Rhonda knew calling them Mr. and Mrs. was instilled in Rusty. They were all adults now. She would have been more comfortable on a first name basis.

She turned her thoughts back to what had been unspoken up until now. She had a sinking feeling. Something was wrong and the expression on Rusty's face confirmed her apprehensions.

While the auditorium still buzzed with youthful conversation, both couples followed Rusty out into the hallway and down to the door leading to the backstage dressing rooms.

"I was pleased when they told me you were going to be chaperoning. Both Billy and I were looking forward to seeing you tonight, but not this way."

"What are you saying, Rusty?" Rhonda questioned.

The young man turned back to face her. The look in his eyes confirmed her earlier apprehensions. Something was terribly wrong.

"We heard you're working for the Sheriff's Department, Mrs. Pohs."

"Please call me Rhonda," she interrupted.

"I will, Rhonda. After the show, Billy was going to have you brought backstage because of the death threats he's been getting."

"Death threats?" Jen echoed. "Who would be sending Billy death threats?"

"That's what we were hoping to find out. When I went into his dressing room, I found…"

Rusty's voice cracked and Rhonda noticed tears in the green eyes. "What happened, Rusty?"

"It's Billy. Maybe you should see for yourself."

Rhonda's mind ran crazy with thoughts of what was wrong. She watched as Rusty turned and opened the door to the dressing room. There was a makeshift sign on the door indicating it was to be used by Billy Roller, complete with a giant star and his name written in block letters.

Hoping for the best and anticipating the worst, Rhonda stepped into the room. Immediately, she could smell the odor of spilled blood and death. Billy lay slumped over the dressing table with a knife protruding from his back. On closer inspection, Rhonda could tell the knife had been stuck in his back after he was dead. Before finding its final resting place, the knife had been used to cut Billy's throat.

"Oh my god," Mark said, his voice hardly louder than a whisper. "How in the hell did you stay so calm when you came out to get us?"

It took a moment for Rusty to regain his composure. When he did, it was evident, he was using every ounce of strength he had to be able to speak.

"Billy and I have been best friends since kindergarten. Neither of us took the threats seriously. Then-then I found this. What do we do now, Rhonda?"

"I need to call this in and get the coroner over here along with a forensics team. When was the last time you saw Bill alive?"

Rusty lowered his head. "It-it was this afternoon at his wedding."

"Wedding?" Rhonda and Jen asked in unison.

"Billy has been going at it hot and heavy with Connie Williams. Last week Connie told him she was pregnant. Billy was over the moon about becoming a father. He insisted on getting married as soon as we arrived in Vegas."

"Didn't the two of you listen in health class when I emphasized using a condom until you were married and ready to start a family?" Mark asked.

Rhona could hear the anger mounting in his voice.

"He always did, but it must have broken, leaked or something."

"None of that matters now," Jen said. "How long has Billy known Connie?"

While Jen asked the necessary questions, Rhonda pulled out her phone and reported the murder.

4

Mark took over the mundane job of closing and locking the door, so no one else would enter the room.

"He met Connie in Sacramento last year. The two of them hit it off right away. They've been tight ever since. To be truthful, if Billy didn't use a condom, she would have been pregnant long before this."

"Where can we find Connie?" Rhonda asked, once she hung up the phone.

"She wanted to come, but Billy said no."

Knowing Connie would not be able to shed any light on what went on here she went on to another line of questioning. "Who has access to this room?" Rhonda probed.

"That's just it, being at a school, it's not as secure as when we play at one of the hotels. Oh damn, what about the show? Billy is due on stage in fifteen minutes."

"For now, only the five of us know what's happened. The authorities don't count. Have the band announce Bill's not feeling well. They can put the show on without him tonight. Until the forensics team finishes with this room, no one is to know Billy was murdered right here at the school."

~ * ~

Mark decided it was best if he talked to the band and make the announcement to the kids. He recognized several of the band members as kids he'd either taught in health class or coached in high school back in Wisconsin. Tommy Baxter had been a star pitcher as well as an accomplished keyboard player. Mark saw Tommy coming toward him and swallowed the lump in his throat.

"Mr. Pohs, Billy told me you'd be here tonight. It's good to see you."

"It's good to see you too, Tommy. I'm afraid you and the band will have to go on without Bill tonight. Rusty came to let me know Billy isn't feeling well. It could be he's caught one of the bugs that's been going around."

Tommy looked worried. "Who's going to break the news to the kids out there? It's not like we can't put on the show, but these kids came to see Billy."

"Let me talk to the kids. Being a teacher here I think I can calm them down."

The look on Tommy's face was one of relief.

Taking a deep breath, Mark walked out onto the stage to confront the students who had been looking forward to the concert, "Good evening," he said into one of the mikes.

Almost immediately the kids became silent.

"I know you came here to see Billy Roller tonight but there has been a bit of a change. The band will still perform, but Billy isn't feeling well. He thought it was best if he went back to the hotel to rest. If it is something contagious, he doesn't want to pass it on to any of you. The band is still here to put on the show."

There were a lot of murmurs from the teenagers. Even so, the kids seemed to take things in their stride and quieted down when the band came on stage. Once they did, Clay Michaels took the mike from Mark.

"We're sorry about you not getting to see Billy, but we plan to give you a great show. Since I know all the songs, I'll be taking Billy's place for tonight. It's not the first time I've taken over when Billy's gotten sick. To be truthful, at one time or another we've all had to step in and help each other. Now sit back and relax and enjoy the show. We promise we'll do our best for you."

By the time Mark returned to the dressing room, the place was buzzing with county deputies as well as a forensics team and the coroner. He glanced at Rhonda, surprised by what he was seeing. "How did you keep this quiet? I never even heard a siren."

"I told them to come without lights or sirens. It's not a life and death situation. The death has already happened," Rhonda replied. "Jen and I will start the investigation as soon as forensics are finished, and the body has been removed. Rusty says he has several of the death threats with him. The ones he can access are on Bill's laptop. The rest of them are at the office he maintains in Los Angeles. Once we clear him, he can fly out to Los Angeles and bring them back so we can go over them."

Mark looked around the small room and saw Rusty sitting on one of the two folding chairs set against the wall. Instead of the mature manager for Billy Roller and his band, he saw the young man remembered from high school. For a moment, Rusty was the kid who wasn't athletic enough to be on the teams but clamored to be accepted. He was the computer nerd who acted as team manager.

"Is there someone you want us to call, Rusty?" Mark asked as he put his hand consolingly on the young man's shoulder.

"This is something I need to do. I need to go back to the hotel and tell Connie what happened. Oh god, how am I going to tell her this?"

"There isn't anything else we can do here," Rhonda said, joining the conversation. "When the show is done, we'll have to tell the band, then we'll go with you."

~ * ~

Rhonda watched from the wings as the band finished the show to a standing ovation from the kids in the auditorium. She ached, knowing in just a matter of minutes she would be telling them the young man who was the cornerstone of their band was dead and his death was far from natural. Someone killed him and until she got further into her investigation, anyone and everyone close to Bill was under suspicion.

"Did you hear us, Mrs. Pohs?" Tommy asked as soon as he saw her standing there.

"I caught a little of it," she replied. "Can you get the band members together and meet me in the rehearsal room?"

Tommy's face went white. "What's wrong? Has something happened to Connie or the baby? Is that why Billy didn't perform tonight? I mean, they just got married and she wasn't feeling well."

"No, Tommy, it's not Connie. Just get everyone together and I'll meet you there in a few minutes."

Rhonda knew she should have confided in Tommy, but it was best to break the news to those closest to Billy at the same time. It was bad enough the man many of them followed from Wisconsin to stardom was dead. As things stood now, every one of them was a suspect and would have to be questioned.

By the time she arrived at the rehearsal room, Mark, Paul, Jenny and Rusty were waiting for her with a young woman who could only be Connie. Rhonda ached for the poor girl. Married for less than twenty-four hours, and now she was a widow with a child growing in her belly who would never know its father.

She was surprised by the number of young men in the room. Beside the band, there were roadies who traveled with Bill. Just seeing the number of people she would need to eliminate as suspects, reminded her of the last case she worked in Wisconsin before relocating to Nevada.

"Thank you for meeting with me. I'm sorry to have to inform you the reason Billy was unable to perform tonight is because he was murdered before the show began."

"Murdered?" Clay questioned. "How, by who? Why weren't we told?"

"Because the show needed to go on," Rusty said, taking the explanation out of her hands.

Behind her Rhonda could hear Connie sobbing, being comforted by Tommy. Taking a deep breath, Rhonda continued. "Billy was stabbed in his dressing room earlier this evening. Rusty found him and came to find us. My partner, Jennifer Sims, and I are homicide detectives with Clark County. This school is in the county and therefore we are the ones who will be investigating Bill's murder. For now, I must ask you not to leave the county as, beginning tomorrow, we will be interviewing each of you."

"Are you saying we're suspects?" Clay asked.

"At this point everyone is a suspect. In an investigation like this one, we need to start with the people who were closest to Bill."

"Even me?" Connie choked out between sobs.

"I'm afraid so. You have my sympathies, but in order to do my job I have to have contact information for each of you. As I said before, none of you are to leave town."

"Can I see Billy?" Connie finally managed to ask.

"I'm afraid not. The coroner has taken him to the morgue for an autopsy."

The statement brought on a fresh onslaught of tears from Connie. The girl wasn't much over twenty and now she was facing a life as a widow as well as a widow of a man who achieved only to be murdered before his twenty-fifth birthday.

Chapter Two

By morning, the media picked up on the story of the murder of Billy Roller and every station seemed to be announcing the news. Most of them were putting up impromptu obituaries for Bill along with videos of many of his performances.

"I can't believe all these stations have this much information all ready. Bill hasn't been dead for twelve hours. The body is hardly cold."

Mark poured Ronda a cup of coffee and joined her at the kitchen table, his cup in hand.

"Bill is big news," Rhonda replied after taking a sip of her still too hot coffee. "I've heard most of the networks have obituaries and films on all of them. Remember how quickly they had information on OJ Simpson and Robin Williams, as well as several others over the past several years. It's the same with Bill."

"Let's change the subject. How did you sleep last night? After seeing that, I experienced terrible nightmares, but whenever I woke up you were sound asleep."

"You need to remember, this is my job, I've been to some gruesome murder scenes. I guess I'm numb to it. It's too bad you and Paul had to see it. It's worse knowing Bill didn't deserve this."

She finished her coffee and got up from the table. "I'm sorry I can't spend a leisurely Sunday with you, but I have a case to solve. I know I won't have the physical letters, but the ones sent to Bill's email are waiting for me to go through them."

As much as Rhonda wanted to enjoy the day with Mark, she left for work. All the way she listened to the news reports of the murder on the radio.

She was grateful no one leaked the information on how Bill died. Beside police personnel, only Rusty knew what transpired in the dressing room at the school and he promised not to talk to the press about what he found.

She pulled into the parking lot and was immediately surrounded by several reporters all clamoring for information.

"Is it true you were the first officer on the scene of Billy Roller's murder, Detective Pohs?" The first reporter to make it to her side asked.

"I attended the performance, because it was held at the school where my husband works, and we were chaperones for the evening."

"How was Billy killed?"

"No comment."

"Do you have any idea who is responsible for the murder?"

"No comment. Look, the case is barely twelve hours old. Give us time to do our job."

"Then you're certain you can solve this crime? Do you have any suspects?"

"No comment."

Tired of being harassed, Rhonda pushed her way through the sea of reporters and hurried toward the security of her office.

"I see you ran the gauntlet," Karl Brannigan greeted her.

"It was to be expected. This is a high-profile case. Did the forensics team come up with anything last night?"

"Not much. There were no prints on the knife, but we're still going over all the prints in the dressing room. I doubt they will lead us anywhere, though. As you know that room has been used by school staff as well as students. If there are no prints on the knife, I doubt we'll find any in the room from the murderer."

"Last night we confiscated Bill's laptop. According to Rusty Phillps, Bill was receiving hate mail. He also said he'd get us the paper copy of letters from Bill's office in LA, but we need to start somewhere."

"There's something else you should know," Karl said.

From the sound of his voice, she was certain she didn't want to hear what he had to say. "What's that?"

"The tox screen came back from the coroner's' officer. Billy had cocaine in his system. We could be looking at a drug-related hit."

"Cocaine?" Rhonda whispered the word.

She thought Bill was as clean as they came. To her he was the kid they'd known back in Wisconsin. Of course, it was entirely possible he'd fallen into the same trap as most people who found instant celebratory status. Big money brought big temptation and the lure of drugs was one of those temptations. One that was too much to resist. Frankly, she'd expected to find alcohol in his system, He just got married and had every right to celebrate. The finding of drugs was a mystery to her.

"Guess it's time for me to get to work on this one. The first people I want to talk to are Rusty and Billy's wife, Connie. I'll arrange for them to come in for a sit-down."

"I'm way ahead of you, Rhonda. Jen got here about twenty minutes ago and left with two uniformed officers to bring them in,"

Rhonda nodded and headed toward her office. This was one case she wished she wasn't involved in. She knew Bill's parents and the thought of talking to them brought a sick lump to her throat.

She'd just finished reading the online threats when Jen arrived with Rusty and Connie in tow.

"Have you found out who killed my Billy?" Connie sobbed as soon as she entered Rhonda's office.

"Not yet, Connie. Why don't we go somewhere more private to talk?"

Rhonda allowed Jen to lead the way to an interrogation room away from the prying eyes of anyone who walked past Rhonda's office.

"Can you tell us everything that happened yesterday?" Rhonda asked once they were seated at the table and the recorder was activated.

Connie sniffed and appeared to be composing herself. "We went to one of the wedding chapels and were married. The band went with us, and Rusty was Billy's best man."

"Who was your maid of honor?"

"That was Sara Trent. She's Jackson's sister."

"Jackson?" Rhonda asked, bewildered by the unfamiliar name.

"He just joined the band two months ago. He plays the drums."

"What happened to Joe Kramer? I don't seem to have time to keep up on all the celebrity news."

"Joe had a problem with drinking," Rusty replied. "He showed up late and drunk one too many times."

"Did Joe hold a grudge against Bill?"

"Hardly. Billy paid for him to go to rehab, and they've remained close friends. He even came to Vegas for the wedding. Even though the wedding was a spur of the moment thing Billy made certain Joe could be with us."

"What about Bill's folks? Were they here?"

"They couldn't make it. After this gig last night, Billy and Connie were going to fly out to Wisconsin. They were planning to have a honeymoon before we were scheduled to be back in Los Angeles. I talked to Billy's parents last night and they will be arriving here about noon today. Tommy said he'd pick them up at the airport."

Rhonda thought for a long moment. "Give me the flight number and the name of the airline. I'll be there to meet them instead of Tommy. I'm sure they have a lot of questions. It's best if we're the ones to answer them. I know Tommy means well, but he doesn't know all the facts in this case."

"What facts?" Connie questioned.

"I'm sorry, Connie, we're not at liberty to say."

"Do you know what she's talking about Rusty?"

Rusty nodded. "For now, I agree with Detective Pohs. It's bad enough Billy's been murdered. You must think about the baby and just leave it at that. I'm sure everything will be explained when they catch whoever is behind this."

Jen continued the questioning, while Rhonda tried to come to grips with this senseless crime.

"What did you do after the wedding?" Jen inquired,

"Tommy reserved a small dining room at the hotel where we're staying. There was supposed to be champagne for everyone, but Billy insisted we all have sparkling grape juice. I look older than I am, so I can get into most bars without ID. Both Billy and I are adamant about no one drinking.

Even if I was twenty-one, I would never risk Billy's reputation or doing anything to the baby. To be truthful, I tried some of my dad's beer when I was a little kid, and I didn't like it. So, I was in no hurry to try anything else. Besides, Billy never drank either, He said he didn't like the taste any more than I did the first time he tried it."

"Where is the detective handling MY son's murder?" The voice of a hysterical woman pierced the air. "I demand to talk to whoever is handling Billy Roller's murder case. I saw everything on the news this morning."

Before Rhonda could question the identity of the woman, Rusty answered the question Rhonda didn't ask.

"Oh god, Lydia Franklin. How in the hell did she get here so quickly? I thought we left that crazy bitch back in Los Angeles."

"Who is Lydia Franklin?" Rhonda inquired.

Rusty took a deep breath before answering, "She contacted Billy about six months ago with some crazy claim to being his birth mother. She said she'd been reading everything she could get her hands on about him. She was certain he was the son she gave up for adoption. We told her there was no way she could be Billy's birth mother; I've known Billy all my life and I would have known if he was adopted. We told each other everything."

"I see," Rhonda replied. "I'll go out and talk to her. She doesn't need to see you or Connie."

Rhonda went out into the hallway, where she was greeted by Karl and a woman of about forty years of age. Her hair was dyed a dark auburn to match Bill's, not her natural coloring. The fake diamond necklace she wore along with the matching earrings set off a low-cut black dress.

"This is Mrs. Lydia Franklin, Rhonda. She says she's Billy's birth mother."

"The title is Ms. I'll thank you to get it right. I want to know who this little twit is."

"This little twit, as you've called me, is the detective investigating Bill Riley."

"So what? My son's name was Billy Roller."

"Billy Roller is nothing more than a stage name for Bill Riley. I've known his family for several years, since we're both from the same town. Now would you like to accompany me into one of our more private rooms to continue this conversation?"

The woman seemed to calm down and followed Ronda to an interrogation room across from where Jen was interviewing Rusty and Connie.

"Now, Ms. Franklin, tell me how you think you are related to Bill?"

"Twenty-Five years ago, I was fifteen and I was pregnant. My parents convinced me it was best if I gave the baby up for adoption. I knew I wasn't fit to be a mother at such a young age. Then Billy became famous, and I could see he was my son. He even looks like my boyfriend, the one who knocked me up."

"What would you say if I told you Bill wasn't adopted."

"That's all hype. I know it is. Even if his parents didn't have the balls to tell him he was adopted, I did. He was mine and I can prove it."

Rhonda raised her eyebrows. "How can you prove it?"

"My son was born on the same day and the same month as Billy. He must be mine. We have the same hair color, and our eyes are the same too."

"If that's so, which I doubt, you won't mind taking a DNA test to prove what you say is true."

"I-I don't think such a thing would be necessary. I know he's mine and that's all that matters."

"I'm afraid you'll have to prove it sooner or later. Why not now and get it over with?"

The woman began to cry, putting on a performance that would have been perfect in a 'B' movie.

"I demand to know how my son died. Was it drugs?"

"Why would you say that?" Rhonda asked, remembering the cocaine found in his system.

"He was a rockstar. Everyone knows they're all into drugs. I just assumed..."

"You know what they say about assumptions, Ms. Franklin. It doesn't matter what you think, I'm not at liberty to tell you anything more. Thank you for coming in. Where can we reach you if we need more information?"

"I'm at the Tropicana. My ex-husband allows me to use his comped room whenever I'm in town."

"Thank you, Ms. Franklin we will be in touch."

Lydia gave Rhonda an indignant stare and got up to leave the room. Before she stormed out, she got in one last jab. "I'm certain we WILL be seeing each other very soon."

As soon as Lydia left the room, Karl entered. "What do you make of her?" he asked.

"She isn't Bill's mother. Of that I'm certain. I know Rick and Sue Riley and Bill is their natural. I'm also wondering how Lydia got here so quickly. What bothers me is she asked me about drugs. Just how much cocaine was in Bill's system?"

"Just a trace. What are you getting at?"

"I know Bill and the band were tested by the school when they first came to town on Friday. It's a prerequisite of the school, not to host anyone involved with drugs. Even the roadies were tested, and all the tests came out as negative. So, in that case, how did he have cocaine in his system at the time of his death? I'm also wondering how Lydia got here so quickly. In my mind, I just added her to my list of suspects."

"Then there's another mystery within this mystery."

"There certainly is. I think I want to talk to Rusty alone."

Rhonda crossed the hall and entered the room where Jen was talking to a distraught Connie and a bewildered Rusty. "Jen, why don't you take Connie down and get her something to drink. I'd like to talk to Rusty alone."

Jen cast her a quizzical look before escorting Connie from the room.

"What do you need to talk to me about without Connie?" Rusty asked.

Rhonda took a deep breath before broaching the subject of the cocaine in Bill's system. "Was Bill into drugs?"

"Drugs? Are you kidding? If anyone in the band was doing drugs, they would have been history, just like Joe. Billy knew our main audience was the younger crowd. He didn't want anything to tarnish our image. Hell, I've never even seen him have a beer during our off time."

"Would you be willing to take a drug test?"

"Me? Why?"

"Because when everyone was drug tested on Friday night, the tests all came up clean. On Saturday night Billy had cocaine in his system."

"Cocaine? Billy? No way. Billy was a straight shooter. Even the hint of anyone doing drugs, especially cocaine, was grounds for firing on the spot. The same with booze."

"Earlier Connie said you were all drinking sparkling grape juice. Why not champagne?"

"None of us like the taste of the stuff. Since Billy was running the show, we all decided on the sparkling grape juice. The taste was better, and it didn't go against any of the rules."

"Were there any distinction between the glasses? Were they served to you, or did you pick them up off a tray?"

"I see where you're going with this. You think the cocaine was put in the juice. If that was the case, anyone of us could have gotten the spiked drink. If the drink was spiked, it would have showed up on the drug test we took after the reception."

"Would you be receptive to taking another drug test?"

Rusty's ruddy completion paled. "I'll do anything you want me to do if it helps find out who murdered my best friend."

Rhonda smiled to think Rusty was so willing to cooperate. Unfortunately, she was no closer to finding Bill's murderer than she'd been the night before.

Chapter Three

McCarran Airport bustled with tourists coming to Vegas for long awaited vacations. Unfortunately, the couple Rhonda wanted to meet weren't here to go sightseeing or hit the casinos. They were here because their son had been murdered. They were here to talk to the detective and claim his body.

This was one meeting Rhonda wasn't anxious to have happen. She was glad Mark was with her. They had been friends with the Riley's for years. Sue and Rick went to the same church as they did back in Wisconsin. She'd also worked on several projects with Sue over the years.

"I don't know what to say to them," she confided to Mark.

"You've done this same thing for several years. I can't believe you're uneasy about this one."

"Yes, I've done it more times than I can count, but never with someone who is such a good friend. Losing a son is bad enough, but how can I tell them about the woman who is insisting she's Bill's mother? Not only that, sooner or later they're going to have to meet their daughter-in-law. When they do, they'll have to come to grips that within six months they'll be grandparents."

"Is everyone convinced the baby belongs to Bill?"

Rhonda smiled at her husband's skeptical question. "I don't think there are any doubts about that. They've been together for quite some time. I think they would have been content to continue dating, but the pregnancy put pressure on for them to get married. She's very distraught, too much so to have any information about the killer. Besides, she was back at the hotel when this happened."

"I'm just saying, I know how kids are today and I don't trust any of them to be faithful to just one person. Last semester we had a bunch of kids who were scoring points by how many partners they could have in a month. Luckily, we stopped it before it got completely out of hand."

Before Rhonda could formulate an answer, she saw Sue and Rick Riley coming toward the carousel to claim their luggage.

"Oh, Rhonda," Sue said, bursting into tears as soon as she reached Rhonda's side. "Please tell me it's not true. My Bill can't be dead."

"I'm so sorry, Sue," Rhonda replied, taking her sobbing friend into her arms. "It's true. We were at the school chaperoning the concert when it happened. Rusty came to get us as soon as he found Bill."

"Do you know who did this?" Rick asked.

Although it was the question most distraught loved ones asked at times like this, Rhonda had to swallow hard, before she answered him. "Unfortunately, it's not like what you see on Law & Order. We can't catch the murderer, try the case, and have closure in an hour segment,"

"I understand," Rick replied, nodding his head. "We're in shock and at the same time, frustrated."

"Of course, you are," Mark said, putting his hand consolingly on his friend's shoulder. "I know this is what Rhonda does for a living, but seeing firsthand what she sees daily threw me for a loop. Did you know about the wedding on the day of the murder?"

Even though she was still consoling Sue, Rhonda monitored her husband's conversation with Rick.

Rick nodded his head. "We met Connie last summer when Bill was playing in Chicago. At the time they weren't planning to get married. Bill called me yesterday morning and said since they were in Las Vegas, they were going to take their relationship to the next level. I urged them to come home for the wedding, but they didn't want to wait to come home. They wanted something simple without all the hoopla their wedding would have generated. I was under the impression that after last night's show, they were going to come home so we could throw them a nice reception. Connie's folks live in Rockford, so we were going to put it on together."

"Did you know Connie is expecting?"

"That was something else Bill told us when he called. He apologized for getting her pregnant before they were married, I told him I know what it's like when you're young and you've found the right girl. I think he was relieved."

The carousel began to move, turning everyone's attention from their conversations to the luggage coming around on the conveyor belt. It came as no surprise to either of them when a bag with a strap reading BILLY ROLLER & THE ROCKERS came around on the carousel. Even in death, Bill's parents were proud of their son and his accomplishments.

Before either Sue or Rick could reach for the bag, Mark pulled it off the conveyor belt. "Where are you staying?" he asked.

"Rusty booked us a room at the Luxor so we can be close to Connie. We talked to her parents this morning and they were booking a flight to come out as well,"

Rhonda cast a questioning glance toward Mark. "We weren't told Connie's parents were due to arrive. Of course, I should have figured as much, but there has been so much going on since last night, I didn't give it a thought. Do you know when their flight is due to land?"

"It should be landing about now," Rick confirmed after checking his watch. "They're coming in from the Rockford airport. Do you have room to pick them up as well?"

"I don't in my vehicle," Rhonda said, her mind whirling for an answer to Rick's question. "It won't take long for me to contact my partner to get here with her vehicle."

Ronda turned away from her friends, to place a call to Jen.

"Did Billy's parents get in all right?" Jen greeted her.

"They did, but Connie's parents are due in any minute, I don't have enough room for them in my vehicle. Can you meet us at the baggage claim area and pick them up?"

"Not a problem. I'm not that far from the airport. I'll be there in about twenty minutes, unless I get held up in traffic. See you there."

Rhonda let out a sigh of relief before turning back to where Sue, Rick and Mark were standing.

"Can your partner come?" Rick inquired, as soon as she turned her attention back to them.

"She'll be here shortly. Luckily, she was close to the airport when I reached her. She'll be able to accommodate Connie's parents in her car."

It didn't take long for Mr. and Mrs. Williams to arrive at the baggage claim area. A young man accompanied them. She decided it must be Connie's brother, as the resemblance was remarkable.

"It's good to see you Jason," Rick said, clasping the man's hand, while the woman hugged Sue tightly before she, too, began to sob. "This is Rhonda Pohs, the detective investigating Bill's death and her husband, Mark. Rhonda and Mark, this is Jason Williams, his wife Pam, along with their son Adam."

"Have you seen our Connie?" Jason asked.

Rhonda nodded. "She's distraught but the members of the band are making sure she's being looked after and protected."

"What about the baby?" Pam managed to choke out.

"Rusty told us she's been checked over by the hotel physician and the baby is healthy."

"Hotel physician?" Jason echoed. "Why not a real doctor?"

Rhonda made a mental note to tread lightly where Jason Williams was concerned.

"Calm down, Dad," Adam pleaded. "If a prestigious hotel like the Luxor employs this doctor, he must have good credentials."

"He does," Mark replied before Rhonda could intervene between father and son. "I know the doctor at the Luxor, and I can vouch for his abilities. He's retired from private practice and enjoys his position with the hotel."

Mark's confirmation of the doctor's credentials seemed to calm down Connie's father. It helped to have their son there to monitor the situation as well.

"Am I in time?'

Rhonda turned to see Jen hurrying toward them. Once Jen was by her side, she made the necessary introductions. "Jen would have been here sooner, but I only knew about Sue and Rick coming to town, until they told me about your family coming as well. I don't have enough room in our vehicle, and it wouldn't be right for you to have to find your own transportation to the hotel. Jen will be taking you to the Luxor. You must understand we have to keep security tight because of the notoriety of this case."

They waited for the luggage for the Williams family to arrive before they went out to the area where the cars were parked. Rhonda insisted Mark should drive and Rick join him in the front seat, leaving the back seat for herself and Sue.

"I have a question for you, Sue," Rhonda said once they pulled out of the airport property and headed toward the strip. "Is Bill your natural son? There's a woman who is insisting she's Bill's birth mother. I asked her to take a DNA test, but she refused. I don't know if there is any connection, but she arrived this morning from Los Angeles. Whether or not she had Bill rattled is anyone's guess. Rusty told me she's been contacting Bill for several months now, but he thought Bill brushed it off as a deranged fan."

Sue sat speechless, but Rick turned to face them from the front seat. "A couple of weeks ago Bill called us and asked for his birth certificate, He said they were thinking off signing on for an international tour, but before he did, he needed to get a passport. After we sent him his birth certificate, we didn't hear anything more about an international tour. We were going to ask him about it next week when he came home for the reception."

"I'm certain he wanted to confirm what he already knew and confront Lydia about it."

Rhonda filed away the information with the intent of asking Rusty what else he knew about the woman claiming to be Bill's birth mother, other than she was probably trying to get money from Bill.

Once they arrived at the Luxor, Rhonda and Jen made certain both families were settled and reunited with the members of Bill's band as well as Connie.

"Have you found my Billy's killer yet?" Connie asked when they met with her.

"I'm sorry, but we haven't." Rhonda replied.

"I don't think my daughter needs you here right now," Jason said, pulling Connie to him in a side hug. "We are planning to get her to the hospital and have her checked out there. Nothing against this doctor at the hotel, but we want to know for ourselves she and our grandchild are okay."

"That's understandable," Jen agreed. "I'll be more than happy to take you to the hospital."

"I'm capable of making arrangements for a rental car."

"We know you are," Jen tried to explain. "Weren't you listening when Rhonda explained the necessity for tight security where everyone associated with Billy are concerned? This is a murder investigation, and we don't know if Billy is the only targeted victim. We have plain clothes officers assigned to guard everyone involved on a twenty-four-hour basis. One murder is one murder too many. We refuse to put either your lives or that of your daughter in jeopardy. That said, I will be escorting you and your family to the hospital."

"Listen to her, Jason," Pam pleaded. "Until we get Connie out of this mess and back home with us, we need to know she's safe."

"Mom's right," Adam chimed in.

The fight seemed to go out of Jason as both his wife and his son confirmed the reality of the situation.

"It's not that we want to limit your movements," Rhonda explained. "We only want everyone to be safe until this case is closed."

Chapter Four

Although each of the band members voluntarily agreed to submit to blood and urine tests, Rhonda waited anxiously for the reports to come back. The excuse the technicians gave that they were backed up was getting old. With no information from the lab, she could do little other than scan through the stacks of hate letters someone in Bill's office faxed over.

Each one seemed to come from the same person, although there were no handwriting samples to compare them to. All the letters were written on a computer, and they all carried the same tone. Each one said that Bill had no right to the fame he'd gained since his appearance on the talent show several years earlier. Whoever was sending the letters was disappointed their chance at fame and fortune never materialized, while Bill was one of the lucky few who made it big.

To try to discover the identity of the person sending the letters, Rhonda made a mental note to call the producers of the show first thing in the morning. She needed to get the names of the other contestants who competed against Bill so many years earlier.

"Why don't you go home and spend some time with Mark?" Karl asked when he entered her office.

Rhonda looked up from the stack of papers on her desk. "I'm just trying to make sense of this one. For me it's personal. I've known Bill and his family for many years. I know I sound like everyone else who loses loved ones, but things like this don't happen to people like Bill."

"Give it a rest, Rhonda. I know how late you worked last night and it's well past quitting time now, Staying here isn't going to hurry up the reports from the lab. It's after six and I'm sure Mark is wondering when you're going to get home."

"Thanks Karl, I'll give Mark a call and let him know I'm on my way. I'll see you in the morning."

Rhonda put the stack of papers into a folder and locked them in her desk drawer before making the call to Mark.

"I wondered when you'd be getting here," Mark said. "Why don't you meet me at Firefly? To be truthful, I've been waiting for your call. Tyson and I are already here waiting for you."

Rhonda smiled. Their good friend Tyson Wrensch had been out of town for several days. It would be good to get together with him again.

"What if I hadn't called and just went home?'

"I know you too well, Honey. When you're working on a case like this one you tend to work late. When someone finally insists you get some rest, you always give me a call to let me know you're on your way. You're very predictable. It shouldn't take you too long to get here. We'll order so the food will be ready when you arrive. We'll also have a pitcher of sangria waiting."

Rhonda agreed. She was a creature of habit. After switching off the light, she left the office hoping to put the case aside for the next few hours.

~ * ~

The Firefly was unusually quiet when Rhonda arrived. Since previously they'd only been there on Saturday nights, she was unprepared for the silence of the bar, as well as the restaurant on a Sunday.

"You made good time," Mark observed, once she was seated beside him at the bar.

"I was promised sangria and good food. How could I not get here as soon as possible? I was also anxious to see Tyson now that he's back in town. That said should we be driving if we're going to be drinking?"

Tyson gave her a side hug as he laughed at her. "Don't you sound like a cop? We thought of that too. Mark and I both came here in cabs. I also arranged for you and Mark to stay at the Tropicana tonight."

"What about school tomorrow?"

"I'm taking a couple of days off," Mark said. "Considering what happened at the school Saturday night, the administration is bringing in counselors to help the kids come to grips with this. I was told to consider this Bereavement Leave since I was so close to Bill. I talked to one of the counselors this morning and they suggested taking a little R&R. I called Tyson and he came out and picked me up. I packed a bag for both of us and…"

"What aren't you saying?"

"I had an email on my work computer this morning. It was a threat by the sound of it."

"What did it say?"

Mark handed her the printout of the email.

Rhonda was shocked to read the words, 'Billy was the first.'

"It's no wonder you're taking precautions. What I don't understand is why you would be a target?"

"We don't know if I am, but I don't intend to make myself one."

"I know you have a hard copy of this, but do you have it anywhere else but on the computer in your office?"

"I forwarded it to my laptop."

"Did you call the authorities?"

"I wanted to talk to you first. This is your case after all. That's also why the school wants me to take some time off. They're thinking of closing the school for the week. We can't take any chances with the lives of the kids. That said, let's try to enjoy the evening. Once we get back to the hotel, we can sort this out. For now, we both need to relax."

Rhonda agreed. There was nothing she could do until they turned Mark's laptop over to the IT department, to see if they could decipher where the email originated. Tomorrow, she would insist a team be sent out to the school to search Mark's desktop computer to see if there were any further emails from whoever was behind this.

~ * ~

The hotel room was almost identical to the one Tyson arranged for them when they first arrived in Las Vegas. As soon as Rhonda stepped into the room, she saw Mark had packed two suits as well as two blouses and hung them in the closet.

"Do you think we'll be here for a while?" she asked.

"I don't know. That's your department. I didn't want to take any chances. Tyson alerted his friend at Metro, and she agreed to bring your car over here so you can have it to drive to work in the morning."

Rhonda nodded. She knew she hadn't had enough to drink at the restaurant to get her a citation for drunk driving, but Mark was right, it wouldn't be good for her to take any chances.

"I'm surprised someone from Metro would do that for us, but of course, this is Tyson we're talking about. There's nothing he can come up with that should surprise me."

She sat at the desk and opened the laptop. She didn't expect to find anything useful, but Mark didn't need to know about her skepticism. After Mark logged in and pulled up his email, she looked at the one he'd forwarded from the computer on his desk at school.

Billy Roller was the first. Schools shouldn't promote dopers. Billy won't be the last. All dopers should meet their maker. Maybe you should start watching your back Mr. Pohs.

Rhonda felt a chill run through her. Everyone knew Billy was as straight as they came. No one knew of the cocaine in his system except for his manager, Rusty. It was one thing they hadn't leaked to the press, just like no one other than Rusty knew how Bill was killed.

"What's wrong, Honey?" Mark questioned.

"Just something no one should know popped up in this email."

"What do you mean?"

"The email refers to Bill as a doper. His image is all about being a straight shooter. I know he was clean on Friday when the band was drug tested. This is just between you and me, but at the autopsy, Bill tested possible

27

for a trace of cocaine. Other than the ME and the officers involved, only Rusty knows about the cocaine."

"How does Rusty know?"

"We asked him to be drug tested because of Bill's results. I thought maybe the sparkling grape juice was spiked. If that was the case every member of the band would test positive. Rusty said he would cooperate with us."

"What did his test show?"

"We don't know because the tests haven't come back yet. I'm at a loss as to how this stuff got into Bill's system. Rusty was adamant Bill wouldn't allow anyone in the band to drink to excess or to do drugs. It doesn't make any sense whatsoever."

"Unless Rusty put the stuff in Bill somehow," Mark said.

"I don't want to think about Rusty being involved. We've known him for years, too. He doesn't strike me as someone who would murder his best friend. Who else would know of your involvement in bringing Bill here to play?"

Mark took a moment to contemplate what she said. She could see him silently debating which side he should take in this debate.

"Anyone at the school would know that. It was common knowledge I suggested Bill come here for a fundraiser at the school. What most of them didn't know was I talked to Bill myself and he agreed to do the show gratis. All we had to do was pay the band. About a week later, I got a call from Rusty, and he said the band heard Bill was playing for free. They wanted to do the same things. No one in the band was making a penny from this gig."

Chapter Five

On Tuesday morning, Rhonda reluctantly went into the office. She knew what she had to do, but issuing a warrant for Rusty's arrest was hard, even though it was the right thing to do. Who else knew the name of the teacher who was the driving force in getting Bill to play at the school.

"Are you sure about this?" Karl asked. "Rusty didn't come off as a suspect in this case."

"I'm not sure about anything, but who else would have sent Mark the email? Rusty knew about the arrangements for the band to play gratis, he was the one to find the body and…"

"…and we need more evidence than what you have. Do you know if the lab tests have come back yet?"

"You know they haven't."

"Do you see where I'm going with this? Bring Rusty in for further questioning. He's been cooperative so far. See what he has to say for himself this time. In the meantime, check with the hotel as to who might have ordered the sparkling grape juice and I'll have the CSI team go over everything from the dressing room again. The cocaine had to come from somewhere."

~ * ~

Rhonda met Jen and together they went to the Luxor to ask Rusty to come down to the office for further questioning.

When the door to the suite where Rusty was staying opened, the look on his face was one of bewilderment.

"It's good to see you again, Rhonda, but something tells me this isn't a social call. Have you found Billy's killer?"

"No, we haven't, Rusty. We're asking you to come down to my office for some further questions."

"Are you saying I'm under arrest?"

"No, but it's always best not to do these things alone."

"You didn't have to bring back-up. You must know I'd do anything to help you find out who killed my best friend."

"I know you would, Rusty. We just have a few more questions and it's best to do these things at the office where we can record it for future use. It's more for your security than for ours."

"Is something wrong, Rhonda?"

She was surprised to see Rick Riley standing behind rusty. "Rick? I didn't expect to find you here."

"I don't know why not. Rusty is like another son to us. We've been giving each other mutual comfort, since the medical examiner's office hasn't released Billy's body so we can take him home and lay him to rest."

Rhonda didn't know what to say. She couldn't tell this distraught father she was here to bring in the number one suspect in his son's murder.

"We're going over everything again, Rick. There have been some further developments in the case, and we need to know if Rusty can provide us with new information. Often what people say in the first interview is not everything. Not because they're withholding evidence, but because the horror of what has happened is too overwhelming. Little things can be overlooked in situations like this one."

"That's understandable, Rhonda," Rusty replied. "I don't know what else I can tell you, but you know I'm willing to do anything I can to help you out."

Rhonda breathed a sigh of relief and realized Jen was doing the same thing. Within minutes they were in Rhonda's car heading toward headquarters.

~ * ~

Through the one-way mirror, Rhonda watched as Rusty talked to Jen. Switching on the sound in the room, she knew Jen was talking to Rusty on his level.

"I wish I could tell you more, but I don't have any idea who killed Billy. If I did, so help me God, I'd be right there to kill the son of a bitch myself. I didn't just lose my job but also my best friend. Maybe I should say my brother. Since neither of us had a brother, we depended on each other and shared everything. Because of one senseless act, everything that was Billy is gone and his child isn't ever going to know what a great guy his father was."

Tears were streaming down Rusty's cheeks and Rhonda could feel the pain he was experiencing. Rather than watch and listen any further, she took a calming breath before she entered the room.

"Do you know of anyone who might have wanted Bill dead?" she asked. "I know I asked you this on Saturday, but sometimes when you sleep on it, you remember things that weren't evident earlier."

"Believe me, Rhonda, I've tried to remember, but other than the threats, I can't think of a thing. You said there were some new developments. Are you thinking I had something to do with it? Is that why you brought me down here?"

Rusty's sorrow suddenly turned to anger.

"We don't know much more than we did before. Who, other than you, knew Mark was the one behind your coming to the school to give the show on Saturday night?"

"Everyone in the band. Those of us who worked with him on the various teams he coached were anxious to see him again. Those who didn't know him were excited to meet the man we talked so much about. Coach Pohs was known to everyone at the school."

"Are there any new members in the band? Someone who has come in recently. Maybe someone resented Bill."

A pained expression crossed Rusty's face. "Just before we left Los Angeles to come here, Billy had to let one of the roadies go. Carlton Axton got mixed up with drugs. Billy caught him smoking pot and told him he had to go. I was with him, and Carlton seemed to be okay with it. He said he was thinking of giving his notice. He knew what Billy's policy on drugs was and he couldn't hide it any longer. I thought we all left on good terms."

"Do you know where he is now?"

"He told us he was going back to Idaho to try and straighten his life out. Billy even gave him the money for the airline ticket and said he'd pay for the rehab facility."

"Did Carlton know Mark had been instrumental in bringing the band to the school?"

"Of course, he did. We were just about to leave when the shit hit the fan and Billy caught him smoking, I can't see Carlton being involved in something like this. We parted on good terms. It's the same with everyone who has ever left the band. Billy was such a good guy, no one held anything against him."

"You said earlier that Billy paid for rehab for Joe Karmer, and now you tell me he paid for Carlton's airfare to get back to Idaho and for his rehab. Has it been like this with everyone who left the band?"

Rusty nodded. "He was generous to a fault. I told him it would be the death of him, and now look what's happened. When I questioned him about it, he said he didn't want to burn any bridges. By helping them out, he knew if he needed something in the future, he could call on them."

A tap at the window halted the conversation. Rhonda excused herself and stepped out into the hallway. Karl was waiting for her.

"I finally received the lab results." Karl said. "All of the other band members, including Rusty, tested negative for drugs."

"Everyone? I thought only Rusty was being tested," Rhonda inquired.

This new information put them back to square one.

"The lab said they all came in together. It sounds like one for all and all for one to me. There is another report you need to see, though."

Karl handed her another folder. As Rhonda read it, she suddenly saw a new avenue opening in the case. Without saying anything, she hurried back into the interrogation room.

"Do you know anything about the candy that was in the dish on the dressing table?'"

Rusty looked surprised. "Of course, I do. Every performer has their quirks about what they want in the dressing room. Billy always requested chocolate covered cherries. They were already in the dressing room when we arrived."

"Did you eat any of them?"

"Good heavens, no," Rusty replied. "I'm highly allergic to chocolate. If I have only one of those things, I'd be on my way to the emergency room of the nearest hospital. My tongue swells up and my throat closes. If I don't get treatment right away, it's lights out for me."

"How does the candy get in his dressing room?"

"It's taken care of by someone at the venue. It doesn't matter where we perform, the candies are in Billy's dressing room waiting for him when he gets in. What does this have to do with anything?"

Rhonda tapped the folder she was holding. "When I stepped into the hall a few minutes ago, I met with my boss. He had the test results from the lab. The first thing I want to know is why all the band members went in to be tested. Did you tell them about the cocaine?"

"All I said was I needed to go in for a blood test." Rusty said. "They said if I was being tested so were they. We went to exonerate ourselves and have whoever is responsible for this caught. How did we test out?"

"All negative. The chocolate covered cherries were another thing entirely. They were laced with cocaine. It must be the way the drug got into his body. Since you didn't eat any of the candy you were unaffected."

To Rhonda's surprise, Rusty burst into tears.

"I kept telling Billy that candy would kill him. I was just joking around. I never thought it would be true."

"You were there, Rusty, you know what killed Bill. It wasn't the candy. I don't know what the candy being laced with cocaine has to do with anything, but we're going to find out. I'm sorry we dragged you down here."

"I'm positive it had something to do with it. Never having taken drugs before, even one piece of that candy would have made him high as a kite. If he wouldn't have eaten it, he would have been able to fight off his attacker."

Rusty's statement made more of the puzzle pieces of this case come together.

"About coming down here, I'm not one bit sorry. You can call on me anytime you want. I'll do anything I can to help you out. I want this case solved as badly as you do."

They no more thana stepped out into the entry hall than they were met by Rick and Sue Riley. The relief on their faces told Rhonda they were ready to think the worst.

"We were so worried when you didn't bring Rusty right back, we asked the officer outside our room to bring us down here," Sue said, her eyes brimming with tears that threatened to fall at any moment.

"You shouldn't have worried," Rusty replied, putting his arms around Sue and embracing her. I remembered stuff I didn't on Saturday night, just as Rhonda said I would. I just hope it helped."

"It certainly did help," Rhonda assured them. "I was getting ready to bring Rusty back to the hotel. Can I give you two a lift as well?"

Rick shook his head, then motioned over to where the uniformed officer was waiting for them. "Don't be too hard on the kid. We asked him to bring us here. He turned us down, but when we said we'd get a cab, he finally agreed. He's a good officer."

Rhonda glanced over at the young man who looked as nervous as a cat in a room full of rocking chairs. Hoping to calm him down a bit, she motioned for him to join them.

"Officer Dickson, I want to thank you for taking such good care of the Rileys. When you take them back to the hotel, would you mind if Rusty rode along with you?"

"No, ma'am not at all."

Rhonda turned her attention back to Rusty. "I know you're going back to Wisconsin for the memorial service, but don't hesitate to call me at any time."

She reached into her pocket and handed him one of her cards, after writing her private cell number on the back.

Before any of them could leave, Lydia Franklin burst into the area.

"I haven't heard one word from you, Detective. What is happening with your investigation into my son's murder?"

"I am investigating the murder of Bill Riley, also known as Billy Roller. He is not your son. It doesn't matter what you think. Sue and Rick Riley are his biological parents, not you, Ms. Franklin. You have no stake in this investigation."

"Didn't you hear me when I told you I gave birth to a baby boy on the same day as Billy was born. I've done my homework. He must be my son."

"I'm sorry for you, Ms. Franklin," Sue said, moving to her side and taking her hand. I pray you will find your son, but Bill isn't the son you're looking for. My husband and I got married because we found out I was pregnant. I gave birth to him as well as his sister. I honestly do feel sorry for you. I couldn't have been able to give up a child for adoption. It was very brave of you. I don't know what I would have done in your situation. Thank goodness I had a man who loved me enough to marry me when I was young and pregnant."

"You are lying. You know Billy is mine. How can you keep him from me?"

The look on Sue's face was one of shock, as though Lydia slapped her.

"How dare you? I'm mourning the loss of my son and you-you are making unfounded accusations. If you're convinced you're my son's birth mother, take a DNA test. You'll see this for the fantasy it is. Just please leave us alone."

The rage in Lydia's eyes was evident to everyone in the room. It was Officer Dickson who restrained her as she lunged at Sue. Rhonda was quick to react.

"Do you want to press charges, Sue? This woman was about to assault you."

"No. I feel her pain, I do want to get a restraining order against her. She's grieving the loss of someone she mistakenly thought of as her son. She needs counseling, not charges filed against her."

As though Lydia hadn't heard what Sue said, she wrenched free from

Officer Dickson's grip by kicking him in the shin. She again lunged toward Sue, but Rhonda stepped in the way, taking the brunt of the assault.

Several officers were quick to arrive and subdue Lydia. "Lydia Frankin, you are under arrest for assault of a police officer," Rhonda gasped when she finally caught her breath. "You have the right to remain silent…"

"I know all that shit, bitch," Lydia interrupted. I watch enough cop shows to know what Miranda Rights are. You'll be sorry you messed with me, and so will they when I prove to everyone they're lying about Billy. He is my son. Do you hear me? My son, and I won't allow you to take him away from me."

Rhonda nodded to the officers holding Lydia. "Take her to a cell and restrain her if necessary."

As the officers took her back to one of the cells, one officer continued to read her the Miranda Rights while she screamed obscenities.

"I'm sorry you had to experience that," Rhonda said as she turned back to Rick and Sue.

"You warned us about this woman," Rick replied. "I thought we would run into her sooner rather than later. I'm glad it happened here, and she was arrested. I would hate to have something like this happen once we got home to lay our son to rest."

Rhonda could see Sue's tears as Rick stated what was more than evident. Had Lydia not turned up today it was quite possible she would have found a way to be in Wisconsin at the time of the memorial service.

~ * ~

"What the hell was going on out there?" Karl asked when Rhonda returned to her office.

"Lydia Franklin came in ranting and raving about how Sue Riley wasn't Bill's mother. When Sue stood up to her, she tried to attack her. She would have if it hadn't been for Officer Dickson. She kicked him in the shin and lunged at Sue again, I stepped in the way, and she assaulted me instead. I arrested her for assault of a police officer."

"That's what I heard," Karl confirmed. "I wanted to hear your version. Jen tells me Rusty told the two of you about a man, Carlton Axton, who Bill had to fire before coming here. Are you planning to follow up with him?"

"As soon as I find him. Bill paid the airfare for the man to return to Idaho. Now, we just need to find out where he went in Idaho. It's a big state, with a lot of wilderness areas. He could have gone anywhere."

"I suggest you find him and find him as soon as possible. He's become our number one suspect."

Rhonda sighed. She was certain finding Carlton Axton would be like finding a very small needle in a big haystack. Her first step was to call Bill's office in Los Angeles. Surely, they would know more about the flight Bill booked for Carlton.

The secretary answered the call on the first ring. It came as no surprise to hear fatigue in the woman's voice. After identifying herself and giving the reason for her call, she was immediately transferred to the accountant's office.

"I don't know how I can help you, Detective," the man said as soon as he answered the phone.

"I beg to differ. We've been told Bill purchased a ticket for Carlton Axton to go to Idaho, I'm sure you can give me the information regarding the flight, airline and destination."

The man signed deeply. "You're right, Detective. This is something I can help you with. Billy booked a one-way ticket from Los Angeles to Boise and arranged for a rehab in Weiser. I checked this morning and found out the ticket wasn't picked up until Sunday morning. I went a bit further and checked with the rehab. They said he checked in yesterday morning."

Rhonda made frantic notes, including the name and phone number of the rehab center. Before ending the call, she thanked the accountant and asked him to feel free to contact her with any further information he might come across.

"I think Jen and I need to make a trip to Idaho," Rhonda told Karl when she finally hung up.

"I thought as much," Karl said, a sound of approval in his voice. "I'll have Jen arrange for you to fly up there tomorrow. Hopefully, this Carlton character can shed some light on this."

Chapter Six

Rhonda and Jen were at the airport for an early morning flight. They'd be arriving in Idaho just before noon and with luck would be able to make the return flight at six-thirty in the evening.

"At least it was a smooth flight without any delays," Jen observed as they made their way to the car rental station.

"I hope the rest of the trip goes as smoothly. Hopefully, we can be in Weiser by two and back at the airport in time for the last flight. Otherwise, we'll be spending the night here."

The drive to Weiser didn't take as long as Rhonda expected. Finding the rehab center was another matter. After driving around the small city for several minutes, they finally found the street leading out of town to the north. The facility was tucked away in a picturesque area at the edge of town.

At the front desk, both Rhonda and Jen showed their badges before asking to speak with Carlton Axton. They were led to a small room, where they waited for Carlton to be brought to them.

"I thought I could smell bacon," Carlton said as soon as he entered the room. "I heard you pigs were here to talk about that son of a bitch Billy. You can save your time, I didn't kill the bastard, but I'd like to pin a medal on the guy who did."

"We are here about Bill. It sounds like you have a grudge against him," Rhonda began her conversation with Carlton.

"Why shouldn't I? The bastard catches me with one joint, and he ships me off to this place, I mean, what is there to do in fuckin' Idaho?"

"It sounded like it was more than one joint," Rhonda continued. "We were told you have a problem with drugs."

"From squeaky clean Billy, marijuana is the road to ruin. I kept telling him I could quit anytime, but he fired me anyway. He said this place would help me quit. What a crock of shit. All they've done is tell me I can't have a joint or a hit of anything to take off the edge of being in this place."

"We were told you and Billy parted on good terms," Jen offered.

"Good terms, my ass. When he says jump, everyone asks how high. I got even with him though."

"How did you do that?" Rhonda inquired.

"Before I left Los Angeles, I went out on one last binge. That's when I got a great idea. I know he likes those chocolate-covered cherries, so I went out and bought a box of them. It didn't take much to lace them with coke. Once I had them, I drove straight through to Vegas. When I got there, I took those candies to the school. I told them I was the front man for Billy, and I got him the box of candies he prefers. They were only too happy to put them in his dressing room. No matter how squeaky clean that bastard wants people to think he is, he had coke in his system when he died. Am I right?"

Rhonda couldn't believe how much information Carlton willingly imparted to them. She excused herself to place a call to Karl, leaving Jen to ask any further questions.

Karl answered on the third ring. "Do you have anything we can use?" he asked, rather than saying hello.

"Carlton admitted to spiking the candy with coke, he vehemently denies killing Bill. We can get him on the drug charge, but I don't think he's capable of murder."

"I tend to agree with you. I'm not comfortable with leaving him in Idaho. It's a rehab facility. He can easily walk away and disappear, I'll get a warrant for his arrest, while you talk with the people there to see if they have a FAX machine."

About thirty minutes after Rhonda called back with the FAX number, the warrant for Carlton's arrest came across the wire.

"Is this what you were looking for?" the director asked as he handed her the FAX.

Rhonda quickly looked over the paper she held in her hand. "It certainly is. We'll be taking your patient with us when we go back to Las Vegas. This is a warrant for his arrest on drug charges."

She could tell the manager wasn't completely on board with her plan, but he didn't argue. "You know what this guy is capable of. Do you think he would be of danger to himself or to us when I arrest him?" she asked.

"I'm way ahead of you. I've contacted the local police department to give you back-up. He's a loose cannon and is addicted to more than marijuana. When he arrived here, he tested positive for cocaine and meth. He's only been here for two days, and the withdrawals are just starting to set in. I listened in on your interview with him and could see the signs of his aggression. It's not that I don't think two women can handle him, but why take the chance?"

He no sooner finished speaking, than two uniformed officers entered the building.

"Do you need our assistance, ma'am?"

"Yes, thank you. I'm certain he will fight extradition, so he'll have to be housed in your jail."

A commotion from the room where Jen was talking to Carlton caused them to rush to her side. The scene that greeted them sent adrenaline shooting through Rhonda's body, forcing her into action.

Carlton had, apparently, snapped and was attacking an unarmed Jen. Rhonda hurried to pull the crazed man off her partner, only to have him punch her, knocking her to the floor. It was the local officers who finally subdued him. Still reeling from the punch, she saw Jen lying unconscious a few feet away from her.

"Carlton Axton, you're under arrest for the illegal use of narcotics," she managed to say, her words sounding slurred from the effect of being punched out.

Before she could read Miranda Rights, Carlton broke free and punched one of the officers. Finally, the downed officer's partner gained control of the situation. Within seconds a doctor arrived and gave him a shot of something to knock him out.

In the distance, Rhonda could hear sirens and soon the room was filled with paramedics. "We need to check you out, Detective."

"What about my partner? She needs you more than I do."

"She's being cared for, along with the other officer who sustained injuries."

Rhonda glanced over to see Jen put on a gurney. "Is she going to be all right?"

"We'll know more when we get the three of you to the hospital."

Rhonda was about to object when she realized her nose was bleeding and her head pounded worse than any migraine she'd ever endured. It happened so quickly she hadn't noticed it before. At the realization, all she could think about was her suit would be ruined.

"I have to call my boss," she protested as the paramedic attached a cervical collar and guided her to a third gurney.

"We'll take care of things, Detective," one of the uniformed officers informed her.

She could see he was holding her cell phone. "Karl Brannigan," she managed to say as the adrenaline drained from her body and she began to shake. Before her vision blurred, she saw another paramedic strapping Carlton to a fourth gurney.

Pain shot through Rhonda's face and keeping her eyes open didn't seem to be an option. Giving in to it, she closed her eyes to shut out the light.

~ * ~

"You took quite a hit," the emergency room doctor said as he reviewed the X-rays. "You have a broken nose and cracked cheekbone. We're going to keep you overnight for observation. Don't be surprised when you look into the mirror. You will have a couple of nice shiners."

"I can't stay overnight. I have a flight to catch. I need to get back to Las Vegas."

"I'm sorry, Detective, but these are doctor's orders."

"What about my partner?"

"She's stable. We're keeping her overnight as well. She was choked unconscious. She'll have a sore throat and her voice will sound strange for a while, but she will make a complete recovery."

"Can I see her?"

"We've arranged for the two of you to have a room together. Once you're settled, the local authorities want to have a word with you."

"I understand. What about the local officer who was hurt?"

"He was checked over and released. It seems you and your partner took the brunt of the attack."

Rhonda sighed. She was thankful the local officer wasn't hurt badly enough to be hospitalized. She knew being interviewed was inevitable. She also knew if she had been allowed to bring her gun to the facility, she could have been charged with shooting a suspect.

She gave into the pain medication she'd been given and slipped into painless sleep. When she awoke, she was in a hospital room with Jen occupying the second bed.

"It's about time you woke up."

Rhonda looked up to see Mark and Karl standing beside her bed.

"How did you get here so quickly? How long have I been out?"

"I was with Tyson when I got the call from Karl. Tyson arranged for a friend of his to fly us up here in his private plane. I was worried sick all the way. When we got here and you were out of it, I worried even more."

"I would have never sent the two of you up here if I thought Axton would be violent." Karl shook his head in dismay.

Rhonda glanced over at Jen. "Should she still be out of it?"

Karl nodded. "I asked the same thing. The doctor told me they're keeping her sedated. From what they told me that maniac almost killed her. It's a good thing you and the locals got into the room when you did."

"How long will they have to keep her?"

"We'll know more in the morning. For now, she's getting the rest she needs. As for you, young lady, I'm putting you on medical leave."

"Like hell you are. I want to know who killed Bill. I know I thought Carlton was incapable of murder, but I do know he was in Las Vegas on Saturday morning. What's to say he wasn't the one who did it? We can't take his word on it."

"The car rental company he used in Los Angeles showed he returned the car to them at seven in the evening. As soon as you told me about him driving non-stop from Los Angeles to Las Vegas, I contacted Rusty. He said, although Axton had a driver's license, he didn't have a car. That was when I contacted the LAPD and they checked with the car rental companies."

Rhonda lay back against the pillow behind her head. "Damn, I wanted him to be the one. He's one mean son of a bitch. Speaking about him, where is he anyway? The last I saw of him; he was being strapped to a gurney."

"He's here in the hospital. They have a prison ward and he's restrained. The doctors think he lashed out because of withdrawal from the drugs he was on. I think otherwise, but it's not my call. We're meeting with a judge in the morning and bringing him back to Vegas with us."

"Is it safe to fly with him?"

"No, it's not. The authorities here are going to drive him back. If Jen can leave tomorrow, we'll be flying back with the pilot who brought us up here. He said he has a sister in Boise, and he can stay with her until we're ready to return."

Karl left the room, giving Rhonda and Mark some privacy.

"I'm so glad you're here," she said, holding Mark's hand tightly. "I don't know how I let him get the best of me."

"From what the officers who were with you said, it was nothing you could have prevented. He was completely out of it, and you got in the way. Thank goodness you'll both recover. I know this is your job, but it's things like this that scare the hell out of me."

"I know I've put you through a lot over the years, but like you said, this is my job. It's what I do. You know how miserable I was when we first moved out here and I didn't have a job. This one is a little rougher than some of the others. At least we know how Bill got the cocaine in his system. I just wish we could charge Axton with murder."

"Since you know you can't, why don't you get some sleep?"

"I thought the local authorities wanted to talk to me about what went on out at the rehab center."

"Karl took care of that. Besides, they had the statement from their officers, and I doubt yours would be much different. Like I said, you need your rest. I promise I'll stay right here until you go to sleep. Karl said he'd take care of getting us a hotel room for tonight."

As much as Rhonda wanted to stay awake and talk to Mark, she could no longer keep her eyes open. The bliss of sleep removed the horrible scene at the rehab center from her mind.

Chapter Seven

The next morning, Rhonda felt as if she'd been run over by a ten-ton truck. Her head ached and her face pounded. She turned over to see Jen sitting up in bed.

"I thought you were going to sleep until noon, Partner," Jen greeted her.

Rhonda noticed how scratchy her partner's voice sounded and remembered what the doctor told her about Jen's injuries when he talked to her the day before.

"I've felt better, but I'll live. How about you?"

"Like you say, Rhonda, I'll live. Did I dream it or were Mark and Karl here last night?"

"It was no dream. When Tyson heard what happened, he arranged for the guys to fly up here with a friend of his. The guy has a sister in Boise, so, as soon as we can be released from the hospital, he's ready to fly all of us back to Las Vegas. Of course, when we get there, Karl's going to put both of us on medical leave."

Jen wrinkled her nose in disgust. "I'm not liking the sound of medical leave one little bit."

"I'm with you there, but you know what they say, you can't fight city hall. Unfortunately, our city hall is our boss, Karl. He's concerned about both of us. I don't blame him, but I had to object loud and long last night. It didn't get me anywhere, but at least I got it out of my system,"

Jen nodded in agreement. "What about Axton?"

"Karl is certain he'll be fighting extradition. They're looking into things this morning. When he's able to be transported, the locals will bring him down in a prison van. I'd hate to have to transport him in a private plane. I doubt he'll be ready to be moved until he's done going through withdrawal. They think it's the reason he snapped. Do you remember anything that happened before he attacked you?"

Jen took a moment to apparently think about her answer. "He was ranting and raving about what a jerk Billy was, then he snapped. Before I knew it, he had his hand around my neck and was squeezing the life out of me. I must have blacked out because the next thing I remember is waking up here with you in the bed next to mine. What did he do to you?"

"I got in the way of his fists. He broke my nose. He also punched one of the local cops. Of course, by the time he got to the local officer, a lot of the fight was going out of him."

For the first time, Rhonda turned to face Jen full on.

"He certainly did a number on you," Jen said, trying to suppress a giggle. "At least I didn't get a shiner out of it. Of course, my throat is so sore, it hurts to swallow, talk and even breathe."

"Has anyone told you when we're getting sprung out of here?" Rhonda asked, pushing past the pain to sound upbeat for Jen.

"The nurse said the doctor would be in soon. She was certain we would be released before noon. I can hardly wait to get back home. More than anything, I want to see that SOB Axton get what he deserves and find out who killed Billy."

"You heard what I said about Karl's orders. Hopefully, with two black eyes, people will be too afraid of me and not even think about withholding the truth from me."

"I have a feeling they'll pity you rather than fear you. From where I'm sitting, you look rough to me. I tend to agree with Karl, but I know where you're coming from as well. I think we need to present a united front to not be taken off this case."

A rap at the door interrupted the conversation.

"Are you girls decent in there?" Karl called as the door opened.

Rhonda looked down at the hospital gown she was wearing and

wondered how anyone could call that decent. "As decent as we can get in these designer hospital gowns."

While Karl went to Jen's bedside, Mark came over to take Rhonda's hand. "I decided you might not want to wear your suit home, so I went out and did some shopping last night. This outfit might not be what you'd pick, but I did my best."

Mark smiled as he handed the bag to Rhonda. "I thought the purple in the top will match your eyes perfectly."

Rhonda took his teasing in her stride, although she resisted the urge to stick her tongue out at him. She pulled the outfit from the bag and noticed the logo. It was a place she regularly shopped in Las Vegas. She knew anything he purchased there would be perfect. "I love everything. I can hardly wait to put them on. Of course, I haven't been told when we're getting out of here."

Looking at the new clothes Mark purchased made her wonder what happened to the things she was wearing yesterday. From what she remembered, everything she brought with her was soaked in blood. She'd even broken a heel when she fell backward.

"I've never shopped for your clothes before. Thank goodness the clerk was very helpful. She said you shop at their store back home, so she was able to get all your sizes correct. I probably would have picked out the wrong size bra and panties. I must admit, I was very uncomfortable in a woman's clothing store."

Rhonda smiled at his confession and quickly changed the subject. "Did someone dispose of what I was wearing?"

"The shoes and hose were a complete loss, but your suit and blouse came back from the cleaner's this morning, and they look like they're brand new. I figured you'd be more comfortable in something a little more casual."

"Boy, how do you rate?" Jen asked.

"She rates as well as you do," Karl said. "I got your size from the clothes you were wearing when they brought you here. Last night I went with Mark, and like he said, we had a great gal waiting on us. This is what she picked out for you."

He handed her the bag with the same logo as the one Mark gave Rhonda. From the bag, she pulled out an outfit almost identical to Rhonda's except for the top being the same shade of blue as her eyes.

Another rap at the door signaled the arrival of the doctor. "I've been going over your charts and there is no reason why you young ladies can't leave today. There are a couple of things I must insist on. The first is neither of you is to return to work until next Monday at the earliest. The second is you need to follow-up with your doctors back in Las Vegas. Mrs. Pohs, your husband gave me the name of your physician and I've already been in contact with her. As for you, Ms. Sims, I'm giving you my contact information to give to your physician, I want to stay in touch with both physicians so I can monitor your recovery. That said, as soon as you're dressed, you're both free to return to Las Vegas. If I can be of further assistance, please don't hesitate to call on me."

"What about our prisoner?"

"He's in bad shape. Withdrawal can be rough, especially for someone as heavily into narcotics as this young man was. From what they said at the rehab center, he didn't check in until the day before you arrived. It takes a while for the DTs to take over a body. I know you're trying to extradite him back to Nevada, but it will be a while before he is stable enough to travel. The authorities have informed me they will be transporting him to Nevada as soon as he's stable enough."

Once the doctor left, Karl motioned for Mark to join him. "We'll go down and finish up the paperwork, so you have some privacy to get dressed," he said.

Rhonda and Jen waited until Mark and Karl left the room before getting out of bed. The night before, Rhonda got up on her own to use the bathroom, but she didn't know about Jen. "Are you going to be okay?"

"I was up this morning while you were playing Sleeping Beauty. A sore throat won't stop me from walking to the bathroom. Why don't you go in and shower first. I'll get my teeth brushed and cut the tags off these clothes."

"I would have given a million dollars to see Mark and Karl in that clothing store. Mark usually lets me off at the door and says he'll be back when I'm done. As for Karl, I bet he turned a hundred shades of red when he had to ask for undergarments."

"At least he was able to get my size from the clothes I was wearing yesterday. You're lucky Mark knows your sizes."

"Weren't you listening when we were talking. I shop at one of those stores back home, so they have all my sizes in their computer database. He was lucky he remembered the name of the store and was able to find one here. At least I don't have to wear that suit and blouse home. I think once things settle down, I'm going to burn the whole damn outfit in the fireplace."

"I agree with you on that one. Maybe we can have a burning of the suits party. I'd say we could do it in our fireplace, but unfortunately, I doubt it would get hot enough to burn everything. It's more for show than for blow."

Rhonda was still laughing when she got into the shower. It felt good to get cleaned up. She knew the hospital staff did their best, but she could feel dried blood in her hair. She had more dried blood on her breast as well as her stomach.

After showering and washing her hair, Rhonda felt much better. Cleaning up didn't help her headache or the throbbing of her cheek, but it did raise her spirits.

Wrapping herself in a towel, she returned to the room so she could brush her teeth and dress in the new clothes Mark brought her.

"I have a feeling Karl must have taken a cue from Mark when he was shopping for clothes. We look like twins, trying to look the same but different."

"I guess you're right, it's the thought that counts. They did do a good job, and I wouldn't want to be wearing the suits we had on yesterday. I'm a lot more comfortable in these clothes."

As soon as they were dressed and ready to leave, a nurse came in with a final dose of painkillers for them to take.

"I gave your husband and your boss prescriptions to fill at the pharmacy, so they should have them when you're ready to leave."

They'd just taken the medication when Mark and Karl arrived with their release forms. With them were two orderlies with wheelchairs. Although Rhonda resented having to be wheeled out of the hospital, she knew it was hospital policy.

~ * ~

Karl drove them to the airport where the private plane and pilot waited. Rhonda didn't like the thought of leaving Axton, but she was also relieved not to be responsible for him on the flight from Boise to Las Vegas,

The plane was a small corporate jet, and she knew she would owe Tyson as well as his friend big time for the convenience. If they would have had to wait for any of the commercial flights, Karl and Mark would have never gotten to Boise until this morning, meaning they might have had to stay in town at least another day before getting home.

"Did you check on Axton this morning?" Jen asked once they boarded the plane and prepared for take-off.

"I did," Karl replied. "The kid is in bad shape. The doctor says it could be up to two weeks before he's ready to be returned to Las Vegas."

Rhonda could tell the medication was taking hold, but she fought the urge to go to sleep. She wanted to know more about the prisoner she had to leave in Idaho.

"What about extradition?"

"He has a lawyer, I talked to him this morning and he assures us he would be fighting it. I think he wants to take his chances on the drug charges and worry about the ones of assaulting an officer later. I don't foresee any problems."

Rhonda stifled a yawn and gave into the medication that was slowly putting her to sleep. As the plane climbed into the early afternoon sky, Mark put his arm around her and she snuggled against him to slip into a peaceful sleep.

Chapter Eight

"Good morning, sleeping beauty," Mark greeted her when she came into the kitchen for breakfast the next morning.

Rhonda was horrified when she saw the time on the digital alarm clock in their bedroom and realized she'd slept until eleven.

"Why did you let me sleep so late? I have work to do."

"To answer your question, you needed to rest. As for work, did you forget you're on medical leave until Monday morning or whenever your doctor here says you can go back to work. Those pain meds you're on are going to keep you grounded for a few days. Since you don't have to go to work, neither do I. I'm planning to pamper you with some great gourmet meals."

"You think so?"

"I know so. We're going back to the hotel for the rest of the week. Karl wanted us to go there last night when we got home, but I told him you'd be more comfortable here for the evening. It gave me time to pack some more clothes. Until this is over, I don't want to take any chances."

"You've gotten more emails, haven't you?"

Mark nodded his head. It was evident he was reluctant to tell her of the one thing she feared the most. Bill's death rattled her. Unlike any other case, this time a murder she was investigating was reaching out to touch her personally. The thought of Mark being in danger made the precautions Karl insisted on easier to abide by.

"We've had police protection ever since we got home," Mark said, overriding her runaway thoughts. Now, once you get showered and have breakfast, they'll be taking us to the hotel. Tyson is concerned, so he's taking

51

time off to be with us as well. What better bodyguard could we get than our six-foot seven friend?"

Rhonda agreed. There was no reason to put their lives in danger. True, they could be tracked down at the hotel, but they would be harder to find than if they were at home.

To change the subject, she asked the question she already knew the answer to. "Have you heard anything from Rick and Sue Riley?"

"I have. They flew back to Wisconsin while you were in Idaho. They wanted time to plan the memorial service to be held on Saturday. They asked if we'd be able to come out for it. I talked to Karl early this morning and he said he thought it would be a good idea. If someone close to Bill is behind this, we might learn something by being at the funeral. I almost laughed, but held it in. I remember how you used to do that when you were working in Wisconsin. Did he know about it?"

"I might have mentioned it, but I don't think he was listening to me. When do we leave?"

"We fly out on the red eye tomorrow night. I talked to Phil Mason while you were sleeping, and he said he'd pick us up at the airport. We're going to stay with Phil and Judy. They'll take us to the airport on Sunday night to catch the late flight back. Tyson said he'd get us the flights with his frequent flyer miles. I told him it wasn't necessary, but you know how he is. He's taking all of this very seriously."

Rhonda thought about the friends they had, both here and in Wisconsin. Phil wasn't only her partner while she worked for the Rock County Sheriff's Office, he and his wife Judy were some of their best friends. It would be good to see them again and bounce the details of this case off Phil. He always had good ideas about things like this when they worked together.

As for Tyson, they couldn't ask for a better friend. When he was in town, he enjoyed treating them to lavish dinners as well as many of the popular shows. Through this investigation, he'd become a rock for Mark to cling to while she worked the case.

Setting the thoughts running through her mind aside, she decided to take her shower and get dressed before having brunch, as it was far too late for breakfast. Once she finished getting ready for the day, Mark served her one of his special weekend breakfasts.

"You look really cute with two black eyes," he teased, as she tasted her fruit topped waffle.

"I look like I'm made up for Halloween. I know the swelling will go down and the bruises will go away. I doubt the memory of seeing that bastard trying to kill Jen will ever go away."

Before Mark could respond, Rhonda's cell phone rang. "Pohs here," she answered.

"Where are you, Rhonda?" Karl greeted her.

"We're just finishing breakfast and getting ready to leave for the hotel. I would have thought your watchdogs were keeping you informed about our whereabouts."

"They were, but something happened on the strip. All units were called to a hostage situation. For now, you're on your own. I'd feel better if you were already at the hotel. Of course, I had another reason for calling. Our IT department has been working on the emails Mark has been getting. It appears the school's computer system has been hacked. The messages have been coming from different Internet cafes around the area. Mark will be able to go back to work next week."

They talked for several more minutes before Rhonda finally ended the call.

"What was that all about?" Mark asked.

Rhonda repeated her conversation with Karl almost verbatim. For the first time she saw fear in her husband's eyes.

"I thought they were going to take us to the hotel."

"Change of plans. I'm sure Karl will make certain our vehicle gets back home after we leave for Wisconsin. For now, I think we should leave for the hotel. Thank goodness you had everything packed before I got up. Another good thing is that no one at your school was responsible for the emails. The computers were hacked, and the emails weren't sent from the school."

"That is a relief. I'd hate to think our murderer is someone I know and work with, but what I still want to know is who?"

"I understand, but these things have a way of working themselves out. Maybe we'll learn something at the memorial service."

~ * ~

At the hotel, Rhonda found they'd been moved to a secure floor. Although the accommodations were posh, she wished she could be at home sleeping in her own bed. As soon as they arrived, their vehicle was taken to a secure lot, and they found Tyson waiting for them in the lobby.

"You look rough my friend," Tyson said after shaking Mark's hand and hugging Rhonda. "I heard about the black eyes and brought you a little present."

He handed Rhonda a gift-wrapped box. As soon as she opened it, she saw a beautiful pair of designer sunglasses that would disguise her black eyes.

"Everyone will think you're a celebrity rather than a hard-working cop," Mark teased.

"I think I like looking like a celebrity. To be truthful I was going to stop at the gift shop and see if I could pick up a pair of sunglasses. With this headache, the lights hurt my eyes and my vanity doesn't want me to be seen looking like a racoon. Thank you so much, Tyson. I will wear them with pride, and I promise not to lose them."

Her statement brought laughter from both guys. Even she realized the humor in her statement. In the past she'd been known for misplacing things, like her sunglasses, gloves and keys.

The suite was beautiful, and the hotel sent them a fruit basket. In the bathroom, she found a jetted spa tub as well as a walk-in shower that would accommodate both of them, if time allowed for such a pleasure.

She did, indeed, feel like a celebrity. If they could have stayed here for the weekend, she would have enjoyed the luxury. Instead, she had to think about the red eye flight they'd be taking to Wisconsin and their reunion with Phil and Judy.

She didn't know if she was ready to go to the memorial service, but understood the necessity of her presence, not only to move the case forward, but to give comfort to Rick and Sue.

Chapter Nine

The two days at the hotel were filled with more pampering than Rhonda ever experienced before. Since the suite had two bedrooms, Tyson took up residency in the second one as their unofficial bodyguard.

They did go down to the gourmet restaurants for meals and while Rhonda went upstairs to rest, Tyson and Mark played the poker slots. They went to a show on the first night, but Rhonda found she was far too tired to think about doing anything else that evening.

Karl called on the second day and said the lab reports were back. There were no prints found on the knife, with the blood belonging only to Bill. Any lead they might have had was a complete dead end.

Rhonda worked on difficult cases before, but this one was personal. She'd known Bill Riley for more years than she could count, He was one of the kids who grew up in her town and was coached by Mark. This entire case seemed as though she was investigating the murder of a family member.

She didn't know what they would have done without Tyson. He'd been a rock and even decided to accompany them to Wisconsin. At first, he insisted on staying with relatives in Watertown, but Phil and Judy immediately said they wouldn't hear of him staying anywhere but with them. Their argument was that, with the notoriety of the memorial service, driving from Watertown would not only be difficult because of all the traffic, it would also be too time consuming, as Tyson wanted to continue his role as bodyguard.

The usually hectic Las Vegas airport was eerily deserted. There were several people at their boarding area, but otherwise it seemed as though the place was closed for business.

"At least they have slot machines to occupy our time." Tyson quipped while they waited to board their flight.

Rhonda saw Mark's eyes light up at the mention of gambling. She knew he enjoyed playing the slots but was pleased with the knowledge he knew his limits. As it was, he'd won over five hundred dollars playing the slots these past two days. If it gave him pleasure, why not? It wasn't a habit and their staying at the hotel was more like a vacation than a security precaution.

She didn't know what strings Tyson pulled, but they were seated in the bulkhead section of the plane. It certainly gave them more leg room. Of course, with his frequent flyer miles paying for the trip, she had no doubt he was able to get preferred treatment.

The flight was surprisingly full. Due to the lateness of the hour, most of the lights were dimmed and Rhonda allowed the painkillers to lull her to sleep. To be truthful, she barely remembered the flight taking off. Her dreams were vivid and filled with memories of finding Bill in the dressing room and Jen fighting for her life. It came as a relief when Mark touched her shoulder to gently bring her back from the depth of dreams and sleep.

"We're about to land," he whispered.

She sighed deeply and licked her now dry lips. "Do I have time to use the rest room?"

"Sorry, I should have thought of that and woke you earlier. We're already starting our descent. We should be deplaning in about fifteen to about twenty minutes."

Rhonda nodded. She knew the restroom could wait. She was anxious to see Phil and Judy again. Thankfully, they checked the weather before leaving Las Vegas. Tyson insisted they stop at the house and pick up jackets to wear over their sweaters. While the weather in Vegas was mild, the temperatures in Wisconsin were still in the low to mid-forties. Considering the flight was landing at five in the morning, she knew the sun wouldn't be up to warm the springtime air.

~ * ~

After deplaning, Rhonda made her way toward the baggage claim area, in the Milwaukee Airport, flanked by Mark and Tyson. After the three-and-a-half-hour flight it seemed as though the baggage claim area was miles away from where they'd entered the terminal.

She heard Judy calling her name before she saw her friends waiting for them. "Over here," Judy called to them.

Rhonda was soon enfolded in Judy's arms, while Phil pumped Tyson's hand.

"Now that's what I call true friends," Tyson said once the introductions were made. "Anyone who gets up and drives over an hour to pick you up at five in the morning is worth hanging onto."

"Rhonda is the best partner I ever had. I'm just glad we were about to not only come here at five in the morning but to let the three of you use our spare bedrooms."

He turned to Rhonda and looked at her skeptically. "He got you good, didn't he? Those are two good looking black eyes. I hope you got in a punch or two."

"I didn't get the chance. I was flat on my back when the lights went out. The last I knew he was in a rubber room going through the DTs. As soon as he finishes with that, he'll be transported back to Vegas. Not only did he lace Bill's candy with cocaine, but he hit me, so they sued him for assaulting an officer. He's also being charged with attempted murder for strangling my partner."

"Thank God the two of you are all right. With all the officers being killed in the line of duty these days, I'm glad I'm no longer on the street. Not that there aren't always threats but I'm not out there with the people who are killing officers for fun or because they make a traffic stop."

Once Mark and Tyson retrieved their luggage, they made their way out to where Phil's van was parked.

"What's the word around town about this?" Rhonda asked once they left the airport behind and were on the highway.

"Everyone is in a state of shock," Judy replied "Some people, and I have a feeling you could name them, say it's your fault. Let's face it. You were in the same town and the same building. Like anyone could have stopped what happened behind closed doors. You should be prepared for what people are saying."

"Have you seen Rick and Sue since they got home?"

"Phil and I picked them up at O'Hare when they got in the other day. They were shaken, especially when the reporters were waiting for them in the baggage claim area. We were glad they called us to pick them up. Phil just flashed his badge and waved them off. Reporters certainly are a vicious bunch. We ran into them again when we got to Rick and Sue's house. A group of reporters were camped out on the front lawn. We didn't even drop them off. We took them to Sue's sister's place. They've been staying there ever since."

"Don't forget about the news coverage," Phil added.

"Oh, yes, it's been on the news steady since it happened. When the story first hit, Rick and Sue's front lawn was filled with flowers from Bill's hometown fans. Then people began arriving. There's not an empty hotel room in a fifty-mile radius, I'm afraid the memorial service is going to be a circus."

Rhonda contemplated the situation they were getting into. The idea of having Mark, Phil and Tyson with her was comforting. As the lead detective, she was a prime target of the press. She knew Jen was laying low in Vegas and she should be doing the same thing. Unfortunately, she was never one to hide out. With the request from Rick and Sue to be present she couldn't say no. In the past, going to funeral visitations as well as funerals had been beneficial. Maybe the same would be true this time.

She knew this was going to be the hardest one she'd attended. Not only had she known the deceased, but not having a body would be rough. Although it was released earlier in the week, it had been Bill's wish to be cremated. Connie, along with Rick and Sue, agreed they would have the ashes buried at an undisclosed date to avoid the press.

Rhonda's head was pounding by the time they arrived at Phil and Judy's house. All she wanted to do was take some pain meds. Once they took hold, she would be more than ready to go to bed and sleep for a couple of hours.

As soon as they pulled into the driveway, she saw the news trucks parked in front of the house as well as several other houses on the street. Even pulling directly into the garage was impossible. The area in front of the door was now occupied with newsmen and cameras.

When the car door opened, reporters rushed forward, carrying handheld microphones. "Detective Pohs, can you tell us if you've found the murderer yet?"

"Are you here because you've been pulled off this case?"

"Do you know if any of Billy's band are in danger?"

"Is it possible the murderer has followed you here?"

"Let me handle this," Tyson said, getting out of the car before Rhonda could join him in the driveway.

"Ladies and gentlemen, Detective Pohs is here to pay her last respects to Bill Riley and to be here for his family. She and her husband are personal friends with the Riley's. We've had an all-night flight, and we need to rest. Detective Pohs is on sick leave because of the injuries she suffered while investigating this case. She has not been pulled from the case, just ordered by her doctor and her superior to rest."

To Rhonda's surprise, the reporters backed off and allowed them to enter Phil and Judy's garage.

"It looks like you've had to handle reporters before," Phil commented.

Tyson smiled and winked at Rhonda. She knew his background. He'd handled the press in the past when he'd helped to solve a murder after having to deal with his so-called best friend stealing his identity.

"Once or twice. It's always the same. They're out to get the big story and today the big story is the death of Billy Roller. Tomorrow, who knows what it will be. Once the memorial service is over, they'll be on to the next story in the next town."

To Rhonda's surprise, the smell coming from Judys kitchen was out of this world, as her grandmother used to say when she liked something. "How in the world did you manage to fix breakfast for us when you came into Milwaukee to pick us up?"

As soon as they walked into the kitchen, Rhonda answered her own question without Judy saying a word. Kitty Redman and Donna Kelly were taking an egg casserole out of the oven and arranging muffins on serving plates.

When the two women saw Rhonda enter the room, they finished what they were doing and hurried over to embrace her. Several years earlier, when she'd been on the Milton City Police Force, Rhonda worked on her first murder case involving Kitty's husband and Donna's father. The two women, along with Donna's sister-in-law Loretta, now ran a successful bed and breakfast in the restored mansion where Kitty and her husband, Karl Reedman once lived.

"Loretta wanted to come over today and help, but she's busy with taking care of our guests. Once they check out, she wants to come over and see you."

Kitty's words were comforting. During the ordeal of the investigation of Karl Reedman's death, Rhonda became close with all three women. Moving to Las Vegas meant leaving the women she called friends behind.

"It's so good to see you here," Rhonda said, unable to hold the stress filled tears at bay.

"You were there for us when we needed you," Donna commented. "It's the least we can do for you now. The whole town is in a state of shock over what happened to Bill. I think everyone is relieved to know you're the detective handling the case We all know you're the person to crack it."

"On this one I'm not so sure. I'm on sick leave for the next few days then who knows what will happen?"

"Phil told us about the assault," Kitty admitted. "Maybe it's a good thing you're taking a few days off. It might be just what you need. Back when you were investigating my husband's murder, you and Mark were so good to me. It's time I'm finally able to give something back to you. Now sit down. The casserole is ready and it's best if it's eaten while it's hot. After that we have strict instructions to get you into bed for a well-deserved nap."

Rhonda sat down at the table, suddenly feeling the fatigue threatening to take over her body. Even though she'd slept through the entirety of the flight, she knew it wasn't the restful sleep she needed.

One bite of the breakfast casserole and Rhonda knew why The Reedman Inn attracted so many guests. The eggs tasted delightful, and the muffins were some of the most delicious she'd ever eaten.

Chapter Ten

On the morning of the memorial service, Rhonda took great care with her makeup. The bruises were fading so she hoped she could cover them up with foundations. After several minutes spent looking into the well-lit bathroom mirror, she had to admit defeat. No amount of foundation would make them disappear. Instead, she looked like one of the hookers on The Strip, with makeup caked on with a putty knife.

Out of exasperation, she ran the hot water into the sink and washed off her attempt to cover up her black eyes. She'd go with the sunglasses she'd been wearing since returning from Idaho.

"Are you okay?" Mark called from outside the bathroom door.

"I'm fine. I can tell you one thing; I'm not used to putting on makeup."

The door opened and Mark came into the bathroom.

"I have a feeling you looked a bit like one of the hookers we see on the street in Vegas. I doubt you would make it on The Strip after all. I'm glad I didn't have to see it, I like you the way God made you, without makeup soiling your natural look. Even if you do look a bit like a raccoon."

"I should hit you for that comment, but I'm afraid you're right. I never have been one to use much makeup and trying to use it to cover up the bruises is rather silly. People know what happened, or at least they should, since it's been in all the papers. Besides, this is our hometown and if they can't accept us no matter what, who can?"

After gently scrubbing the makeup from her face, she applied moisturizer and a little lipstick. Pleased with her appearance, she went into the living room to join the others.

"Mark said you thought you looked like you should be on The Strip," Tyson teased. "It's too bad you had most of the makeup off when he came into the bathroom. I would have given anything for him to have snapped a picture of you with his phone."

"It's a good thing he didn't," she retorted. "I'd hate to have to arrest him for harassment."

Everyone laughed at her comment, taking the edge off where they would be going this afternoon.

Rhonda looked at the vertical blinds that were now closed. She knew it could only mean the press was still lurking outside the front door.

"Are you ready to leave?" Phil asked.

"As ready as I'll ever be. Going to these things never gets easier. This one is especially bad, considering we all knew Bill so well."

~ * ~

Because of Bill's notoriety, the service was held in the high school gym where Rhonda used to watch Bill play so many basketball games when he was in high school. Big flat screen TVs now played a slide show of Bill Riley's life along with videos of his shows.

The press was set up in the parking lot, as the family asked not to have any cameras allowed inside during the service.

The band members, along with Connie, stood with Rick and Sue in the receiving line. Someone had hung banners from the basketball hoops saying WE LOVE YOU, BILLY. Rhonda was certain it had been done by his teenage fans.

She was greeted by several old friends including her first boss in law enforcement, Jack Franks, and Sheriff Cantwell from the county sheriff's office.

"It's good to see you Rhonda," Jack said. "I wish circumstances were different. I can't believe something like this could happen to a great kid like Bill. I watched him play a lot of games in this gym."

"I know, I'm still trying to wrap my head around what happened, while I'm trying to solve this case. Thank God Mark and I were at the school and were the first ones on the scene. My partner, Jen, was there as well. I just don't know where this one is going. There have been a lot of false leads, but we'll find out who is behind this eventually."

"I haven't told you before, but I am proud of the officer you've become. I never thought things would go so well for you when I hired you as a grief counselor. You've got the makings of a topnotch police officer. Your superior better watch his step, because I have no doubt, you'll be up for his job sooner rather than later."

Rhonda was humbled by what Jack said. When she worked for him, she was the token female officer, the least likely to do anything noteworthy. She knew he'd been shocked when she solved the biggest case in the history of their small town. It meant the world to hear him say he was proud of her.

They moved forward in the line and were getting closer to being able to speak to Rick and Sue when she realized she wasn't paying attention to the people around her. There were too many for her to be able to focus on individuals.

For some reason, Rhonda couldn't take her eyes off Connie, the supposed grieving widow. It was always hard to see the grieving spouse, but she couldn't get a read on Connie. She'd only been Bill's wife for a matter of hours, but they'd been together for longer than that, especially considering she was obviously pregnant. There had been so much going on in Las Vegas, Rhonda hadn't been so acutely aware of the girl's condition. Now she could see the beginnings of a baby bump under the dress Connie wore with its too-short miniskirt.

Rhonda didn't know what to make of the girl who stood dry-eyed next to the parents of her dead husband. Pictures of Bill kept showing on the screens with only a minimum number of pictures of Connie. Rhonda wondered if it was to keep her away from the press or something else.

The one picture that caught Rhonda's eye was apparently taken at the wedding several days earlier. Connie was wearing the same dress she was in today and looking adoringly into Bills eyes. It was the man standing behind them, apparently in an attempt to photo bomb them, that bothered Rhonda.

She knew he wasn't a band member, so who was he? The picture was followed by an official wedding photo, minus the photo bomber.

She stopped watching the monitor when she found herself next in line to pay her respects to Rick and Sue. Rick pulled her into a bear hug and accepted her words of sympathy. It was Sue who not only hugged her but cried desperate tears.

"I don't know how we are going to go on without Bill. He was the light of our lives. I'm sure you know we lost his sister to cancer three years ago. He was all we had left."

"I understand, but you do have a lot to look forward to. When Connie gives birth, you'll have a precious grandchild to love. That's something special that will be happening in your life. Just remember God never closes a door without opening a window."

Sue didn't reply, but Rhonda thought she was acting less than enthusiastic about the upcoming birth of her grandchild. What had happened between Sue and Connie between when they talked in Las Vegas and now?

With so many people behind her, Rhonda knew she had to move ahead. Before doing so, she whispered to Sue that they would talk later.

Connie took Rhonda's hand and gave her the limpest handshake she'd ever experienced. "Do I know you?" Connie asked.

The girl's question caught Rhonda off guard. It was doubtful she would know any of the people who were at the memorial service beside her parents, brother, and the band members. She also had to know who Rhonda was considering she was investigating the murder of her husband.

"I'm Detective Pohs. We talked when we were in Las Vegas. I'm sure you remember."

"Oh yes. It's been such a trying time and I've had to meet so many people today. They all blur together after a while. It's hard to keep everyone straight."

"I may want to talk to you again in the future," Rhonda said.

It was evident it didn't faze the girl any more than all the pictures of the man she'd married and lost in such a short time.

"I'll be staying with my parents," Connie replied, after pausing as if to decide what to say.

Rhonda nodded and moved on. She exchanged pleasantries with Bill's grandparents before seeing Rusty coming toward her.

"I'm sorry for what Carlton did to you. I didn't know he was addicted to the hard stuff. I hope he gets help. I just can't believe he was the one who put the cocaine in the candy in Billy's dressing room."

Before Rhonda answered, she considered Rusty's use of the name Billy. She always thought of him as Bill, but thinking back, the kids Bill hung with always called him Billy. It was only natural that he would take that nickname and turn it into his stage name.

"He admitted to it," she finally answered. "It was just before he tried to strangle my partner. I know he was a friend of yours, but he wanted to have Billy caught with cocaine in his system to ruin his reputation. I don't understand the mentality of the people who are on drugs, but they do get strange ideas in their heads."

"It still doesn't seem right. He traveled with us for over a year. I didn't think he'd be cruel enough to want to tarnish Billy's image. He knew when he signed on with us how Billy felt about drugs and alcohol. Everyone signed papers saying they understood the rules."

"It doesn't matter now. We have records from the car rental company that puts him back in Los Angeles at the time of the murder. I have another question for you, though. Can you get me a copy of the picture of Bill and Connie at their wedding? Not the official one, but the picture before that."

'Sure. I put the pictures from while we were on the road on a thumb drive. Why are you interested in that picture?"

"I want to know who the guy is who photo bombed them."

"I hadn't noticed him before. I guess I was concentrating on the picture of Billy and Connie. He looks familiar, but I can't put a name to him. It could have been someone from the hotel while we were celebrating the wedding. You know how people are, they always want to photo bomb celebrities. It happened all the time to Billy."

"I'd like to take a copy of the picture to the hotel and see if someone there can identify him. He seems to be especially close to Connie, wouldn't you say? If I was photo bombing a celebrity, I'd be closer to him than to someone I didn't know from Adam. I'll be in town until tomorrow night. We're staying at Phil and Judy Mason's. I'm sure you remember where they live."

"I do. Their son Sean was in our class. I was over there a lot when I was a kid. I'll get the pictures to you tomorrow, including some others I have on my computer. It's possible this guy photo bombed us before. I can't be sure, though. There are always so many people around when we do a show, and everyone wants a picture with Billy."

Rhonda thanked Rusty and went to where Mark and Tyson were seated and waiting for her.

"What was that all about?" Mark inquired.

"Have you been watching the slide show?"

Mark's expression was one of bewilderment at her question. "Sort of. I was paying more attention to talking to old friends. Did I miss something?"

"It's possible you did. It's a good thing they keep playing the pictures over again. There's a picture of Billy and Connie at the party after the wedding and some guy who didn't belong was standing behind them. Rusty thought he looked familiar but couldn't put a name to the face. He's going to bring over copies of the pictures from the time they first started on tour until the wedding, I want to see if he photo bombed them before. Maybe I'm being paranoid, but at this point anything is worth a shot."

"It wouldn't be the first time you've gotten leads off pictures," Mark observed. "I hope it helps. The longer this one is open, the more I worry about you."

"You're sweet, Honey, but I worry about you as well. I'm not sure you should be returning to work on Monday. I know you've been getting more threats through your email."

"I'll be fine. I promise. We've ascertained none of the emails have been coming from the school, but someone who hacked into our computer system. It's all been resolved and the IAT department from the county has been setting up better firewalls. I'll be just as safe at school as you are on the job."

"I think that's a bad comparison, buddy," Tyson said. "From what I've seen, Rhonda isn't exactly safe when she's at work."

Even though it wasn't meant to be funny, everyone laughed to relieve the tension of the moment. Tyson was right. She wasn't always safe at work. The episode in Idaho attested to that.

The line of people coming to pay their respects finally ended and people took their seats for the service. Throughout the congregation teenage girls cried loudly. It was Connie who caught Rhonda's attention. She wasn't playing the part of the grieving widow well. While Bill's parents cried bitter tears, Connie sat dry-eyed throughout the service, Rhonda knew she would be doing some major investigation work when she got back to work.

~ * ~

The memorial service had been draining for everyone. Although a luncheon was served, Rhonda was too busy monitoring various conversations to fill a plate.

"I see you aren't eating," Judy admonished her.

"I know I should be, but I might find out something by listening to conversations."

"You're pushing yourself too hard. Tyson approached us and he wants to take us all out to dinner tonight. He made reservations for us at the Milwaukee Grill. For now, we all think you should go back to the house and rest."

Rhonda nodded in agreement. Her headache was raging, and she needed not only to rest but to take some of the painkillers.

Before leaving, she went over to speak with Rick and Sue. "We're leaving now. We'll talk after I get back home. I'll keep you updated with everything we find."

"Thank you for coming this far, I know it would have meant a lot to Bill to know you cared enough to make the trip. He was looking forward to seeing you again at the show the night he was killed."

Rhonda wiped the tears away as she hugged both Rick and Sue. She wished she'd gleaned more information from today's service. She planned to solve this one, even if it didn't look likely at this time.

As soon as she left the area where Rick and Sue were seated, she saw Mark and Tyson waiting for her at the cafeteria door.

Before she got to their side, she was stopped by Connie. "What are you doing here? I thought you were trying to find out who killed Billy. It certainly wasn't anyone in this hick town."

"I'm here because his parents are personal friends of my husband and me, I'm also here because I watched Bill grow up. If I get any information that can be used in solving this one, so be it. If not, this is nothing more than paying respects to Bill and giving comfort to his parents. If you haven't heard, I'm on sick leave until Monday because of what Carlton Axton did to my partner and myself in Idaho. As for this being a hick town, this wasn't just Bill's hometown, it is home to my husband and myself."

The look on Connie's face denoted a hatred for Bill's hometown and the fact Rhonda came from Las Vegas for the funeral irritated her even more. The girl rubbed her wrong from the get-go. Rockford was a larger town, but nothing like Las Vegas, Los Angeles or Chicago. She wanted the glitz and glamor of being in the spotlight and now she was little more than a little fish in a big pond. Without Bill, she was nothing more than another single mother raising a child in the Midwest.

"Where are Phil and Judy?" she asked when she finally made it to where they were standing.

"Phil went to get the car," Mark said, holding her coat for her. "It started raining about an hour ago. We're going back to their place so you can take a nap before we go out to dinner."

"Honestly I'm fine."

"I doubt that. I saw you talking to Connie. What did she want?"

"She wanted to blow off steam. I think she's coming to realize she's going to be a single mom and not eye candy on Bill's arm."

Tyson put his arm protectively around Rhonda's shoulders. "I've heard what you're like when you're working a case. Whatever it was Connie said, upset you. I'm going to play Doctor Tyson and prescribe you to go back to Phil and Judy's house and get some rest."

Rhonda smiled at his take-charge attitude. She knew she needed to rest but hated to admit to the weakness. She had a case to solve, and she couldn't do it by taking a nap, even if she was on sick leave.

~ * ~

When Rhonda woke from her nap, it was time to go out to dinner. As much as she didn't want to admit it, she did feel better. The pain meds lulled her into a peaceful sleep and her headache did subside noticeably.

She was surprised to find Rusty sitting in the living room talking with Mark and the others. "I didn't expect to see you until tomorrow."

"I know but I thought there might be other people you wanted to see while you're here, so I decided to come over this afternoon. Since we have all the photos in one folder on the computer, I copied them onto a thumb drive for you. It's easier than printing everything out. I didn't take the time to go through them, but I'll be available whenever you need me."

"What do you mean available?"

"I have business to finish up in Las Vegas as well as Los Angeles. I also need to look for another job. I don't know how many of the band members will be going back with me, but we'll all find our new ways in the world. None of us ever expected anything like this to happen. I think we believed we'd be playing with Billy for the next fifty years. I've already had a couple of offers to work as a manager for other bands. I want to weigh my options and meet with the people that have contacted me."

The thought of Rusty working for another band seemed strange to Rhonda. Here he was home, but over the past several years his lifestyle changed to the point where he was more comfortable in the world of entertainment. It was true he started managing Billy when he was green as grass. Since then, he'd matured into a manager whom others wanted on their staff. He would, certainly, go far in his life surrounded by the glitz and glamour of life on the road.

"How are your folks taking your decision to return to the West

71

Coast?"

"They're cool with it. They were older when they had me so they're planning to retire and move to Arizona. In a few months this won't be home anymore. They were down there for two months last winter and bought property. Of course, they're not thrilled with the summers, so they've also purchased property in Wyoming to use as a summer home. During hunting season, they are planning to rent it out. I'm glad they're doing something they've wanted to do for a long time. Dad wants to be out in the woods and Wyoming gives it to him, while Mom isn't thrilled with the cold winters, so the place they bought in Sun City will be perfect for the winters."

Rhonda could remember spending several evenings with Rusty's parents and knew Ron enjoyed hunting and fishing while Kathy liked fun in the sun. The decisions they'd made for themselves made perfect sense. She wondered if Rusty's plans played a part in it. It was entirely possible he'd contributed to both purchases so his parents could fulfill their dreams.

They talked for several minutes before Rusty left and they could prepare to go out to dinner. Rhonda found she was looking forward to having a meal at the Milwaukee Grill. It was always one of her favorite places to eat and she missed seeing the owners, Mark and Andy. She hoped they would be there tonight and not at their home in North Carolina.

~ * ~

The parking lot of the Milwaukee Grill was filled with cars, making Rhonda wonder if they would be able to get a table. Even though Tyson told them he'd made reservations, she still had her doubts.

She was surprised when Tyson went downstairs to the banquet room rather than heading for the main restaurant.

"Where are you going? The dining room is upstairs."

"I know," Tyson replied, giving her a sly wink. "There were several people who wanted to meet with you, so we decided this was the best way to handle things."

Rhonda was surprised when she walked into the basement dining room. Her former partners Martin and Bob were there. With them were their wives along with Sheriff Cantwell and Chief Franks. Also, there were members of the Adkins and Richardson families. She'd solved murders for each of them in the past. At another table were Donna Kelly, Kitty Reedman and Loretta Reedman. Either they didn't have guests at the bed and breakfast or someone else was taking care of their needs tonight.

"I don't know what to say."

"Don't say anything," Sheriff Cantwell told her. "I know Chief Franks and I gave you a hard time when you first started working for us, but tonight we're all here to honor you. I've heard from most of these people, and everyone wanted to see you while you're here and decided this was the best way to do it. Luckily, this young man contacted me, and I was able to make all the arrangements."

As much as Rhonda would have liked to pick the brains of her former partners and bosses, she knew this wasn't the time or the place. Everyone came to spend the evening with her, not to talk about the current murder she was trying to solve.

"You've got a tough one this time, Rhonda," Sheriff Cantwell said.

They were sitting at the same table along with Chief Franks, Phil, Martin and Bob. They'd all worked with her on various murders over the years and were her trusted colleagues.

"They're all tough. Only this time I don't have many suspects. I thought I had the right guy when I went to Idaho. Unfortunately, he was so strung out on drugs he only wanted to tarnish Bill's reputation. I hope something breaks soon. I certainly don't want this to turn into a cold case scenario."

"You'll do just fine," Chief Franks said. "I remember when I first hired you, I thought you'd be a great grief counselor. You proved me right and surprised me when you solved the Reedman murder. You'll never know how proud of you I am."

"I second that," Bob commented. "I only partnered with you for a short time, but I'm honored to have been able to work with you. I learned a lot."

"I'll say," said Martin. "I never thought about going to funeral visitations to get a handle on the killer. I've done it ever since we partnered together."

As much as Rhonda enjoyed the adulation, she knew there were other people in the room she wanted to talk to.

Once they finished eating dinner, she went over to the table where the Adkins family were sitting. Maggie was holding court as the head of the family, with David and his wife. Virginia and her husband were there and with them were the twins, Rosco and Norton.

It was the same at every table in the room. Each family brought back memories of the murders, bringing them into connection with one another. Even though the wounds were healed, Rhonda knew she was a bitter reminder of the darkest time in their lives.

All too soon, the evening ended. Rhonda knew within twenty-four hours they would be on a plane heading back to Las Vegas and the investigation into who killed Billy Roller.

Chapter Eleven

Monday morning Mark drove Rhonda to the clinic to be checked out. To her disappointment, she was told she could return to work, but only desk duty. Her doctor decided the painkillers were still necessary to relieve the headaches, but driving was still out of the question.

Mark smiled at the doctor's orders. "If I didn't have to work today, I'd insist you stay home, but at least if you're deskbound, I don't have to worry too much about you getting out of line."

"If it will make you feel any better," the doctor said, "I examined Jenny earlier and she's on desk duty as well. The two of you have been through a trying experience and neither one of you is ready to do any driving."

Rhonda knew both Mark and the doctor were right, but she still chafed at being restricted. At least she had the thumb drive from Rusty. Going through the pictures would be time consuming if not boring. It was also something she and Jen could do together.

At the office, Mark kissed her goodbye before leaving for his first day back at the school since the murder, over a week earlier. Although she knew they both needed to get back to their normal routine, she worried about Mark returning to work. Even though they'd been in Wisconsin over the weekend, the threatening emails continued to arrive in his inbox.

Jen was waiting for her at the office. The bruising around her neck was healing, but her voice was still hoarse. "Tell me about your trip to Wisconsin. How did it go at the memorial service? Did you get any leads to check on?"

Rhonda settled into her chair. "One question at a time. The trip was bittersweet. It was hard seeing Rick and Sue so distraught, but I did connect with several old friends. The memorial service was interesting. I couldn't believe how composed Connie was. She was supposed to be the grieving widow and yet, I didn't see her shed a single tear. Everyone else was crying and yet she stood dry-eyed in the receiving line. I don't know how she held up during the memorial service since I wasn't seated close to them. I also think she's further along than we were told. I'd say she she's at least four or five months along.

"As for leads, I found a picture of someone photo bombing Bill and Connie at their wedding reception. I have a funny feeling about him, so I asked Rusty for pictures from the previous six months. He gave me a thumb drive. I used Mark's laptop to make a copy of it for you. I figure two sets of eyes are better than one any day of the week."

"Wow, that's a lot to digest. Do you think Billy knew how far along she was?"

"I doubt it. I mentioned it to Rusty, and he told me he was certain she was only three months along. Bill insisted they had to get married as soon as he found out about the pregnancy. Something else isn't adding up. In addition to that, I mentioned the grandchild to Sue, and she acted kind of funny about it."

"Guess the only thing they can do is wait until the child is born and have a DNA test done."

"That's exactly what I was thinking. In the meantime, I'd like to look through the stuff on the thumb drive and see if we can find him in any of them. Rusty thinks it's a waste of time because fans are always photo bombing Bill and the band. Since we're going to be desk jockeys for the next few days, we'll have plenty of time to look through them, I divided them up, so here is your thumb drive."

Rhonda plugged in the thumb drive and went to the picture she'd seen at the memorial service, so Jen would know who to look for. Before starting to go through any of the other pictures, she emailed it to the IT department so they could make copies of it. Along with the attachment she added a message: *This is a picture I'd like to have blown up and printed. If I come across any other pictures to question, I will forward them to you. Thank you for your help - DRP.*

They spent the remainder of the morning going through the contents of the thumb drives and came up with three others from the time Connie and Bill were dating, all with the mystery man in them. Each was sent to the IT department with an accompanying message.

They were almost ready to break for lunch when Rhonda's phone rang. "Pohs here."

"This is Carla Kline calling from Billy Roller's office. I was going through the morning mail and thought something I received might be of interest to you. I received a copy of Billy's will. It came from his lawyer. When I called him, he said it had been revised on the morning before Billy was killed. He said he wanted his wife and unborn child provided for. With all that happened he didn't come across it until late last week. It's legal and he sent me a copy. Would you like me to fax it to you?"

Rhonda immediately perked up. Maybe this desk duty wouldn't be too bad after all. "Yes, I'd appreciate it. Also, if you have a copy of the first will, I'd like to see it as well."

She gave Carla the fax number. After several minutes, the fax came through. She knew what she would be doing for the remainder of the day. Even though she was anxious to compare the two legal documents, she thought it best if they went to lunch first.

Since neither of them had been released to drive yet, Karl offered to take them to lunch. Armed with the pictures she'd requested from IT, she anticipated an interesting lunch meeting.

They found a secluded table at a restaurant not far from the office, As soon as they put in their order but before they could start comparing the photographs, Rhonda's phone rang.

"This is dispatch," the caller identified herself. "We've just received a call regarding a shooting at your husband's school. My supervisor told me I should contact you."

"Y-yes you did the right thing. I'm here with my supervisor and my partner. We'll be right there."

"We'll be right where?" Karl inquired as soon as she hung up.

"There's been a shooting at Mark's school. We need to get there."

"We also need to get our lunch. Since we ordered sandwiches, we'll get them to go."

Rhonda knew her boss was right. He was thinking a lot straighter than she was. Her mind was reeling with thoughts of the worst things that could have happened. Mark was still getting the threatening emails. What if someone killed him? How would she go on without him?

While her mind spun with thoughts of what if, Karl hailed their waitress and soon their sandwiches were handed to them in Styrofoam containers, as were their drinks. Within ten minutes of receiving the initial call, they were on their way to the school.

Although Rhonda sipped her iced tea, her sandwich was untouched. As much as she enjoyed Rúben sandwiches, she knew it wouldn't sit well until she knew Mark was safe.

~ * ~

Mark pulled into his assigned parking space. He was a bit apprehensive about returning to work. The emails were becoming more and more threatening. Even so, he couldn't spend the rest of his life acting like a scared rabbit. Life had to go on and it was time to get back to softball practice with his team, He also had a ton of paperwork waiting for him in his office.

He'd stopped at Starbucks to pick up a cup of coffee and drove to the school. After parking in his marked space, he downed the last of his coffee. He timed it so he would get to the cafeteria in time for lunch. He'd arranged for a luncheon meeting with the principal as well as several other staff members and people from the school board.

He'd just entered the cafeteria when he heard screams coming from the other side of the room. In front of him, he saw a student with a gun. To his horror, the student pulled the trigger, and a girl went down. Instinctively, Mark rushed toward the shooter. Before he could get in range to stop what was happening, the boy turned the gun on him,

The sound of the gun discharging was deafening. The pain in Mark's shoulder was instantaneous. Despite his injury, he continued forward until he was able to tackle the shooter.

From there things escalated. Other teachers and students were with him, restraining the shooter and taking the gun from his hands.

Someone helped Mark to lie down on the floor and he was more than willing to follow their instructions, He could feel the blood draining from his body and lightheadedness threatening to send him into unconsciousness.

~ * ~

When Karl, Jen and Rhonda arrived at the school, ambulances and squad cars filled the parking lot and her heart lurched. If there had been a shooting, she wondered if it was possible Mark had been hurt. It was one thing when she was the one in danger. It was another thing to think Mark was in the same position.

As soon as Karl parked the car, Rhonda and Jen were out running toward the school, their badges in hand. "What happened?" Rhonda demanded when she was stopped at the door.

"A student brought a gun to school. One student was shot, and the paramedics are getting her ready to transport to the hospital. The only other victim was a teacher who stopped the assailant, the shooter is in custody and the gun has been confiscated. Everything is under control."

Before Rhonda could say anything, the paramedics rushed the first gurney past her. On it she saw a young girl, the stain of blood covering the right side of her chest. She looked pale from the loss of blood. Seeing someone so young fighting for their life, Rhonda felt her stomach churn at the terrible waste when something like this happened.

The first gurney was followed closely by a second. This one carried Mark, his left shoulder soaked in blood. "Mark," she screamed as soon as she saw him.

She felt strong hands holding her up as her legs threatened to collapse. She knew it was Karl who supported her.

"This is his wife. Can she ride with you to the hospital?"

The paramedic looked skeptical but finally agreed. Rather than get into the back with Mark, she was allowed to sit in the passenger's seat. From her position, she watched as the first ambulance left, with sirens blaring and lights flashing.

Rhonda's mind whirled with emotions. She'd been injured in the line of duty, but that was part of her job. Mark had the safety of being a teacher and a coach. Both were safe jobs. He was supposed to be in a position where he could not get hurt. Now everything had changed. He'd been shot and was on the way to the hospital. Even though she knew his wound wasn't life threatening, what about the amount of blood he lost? That would account for how pale he was, but it could be too much. Was he in danger of dying either on the way to the hospital or when he got there? She knew the questions crowding her mind were all without answers until they got to the Emergency Room.

It appeared hours passed before they finally pulled into the ambulance bay at the hospital. It was only a matter of minutes. As soon as they stopped, Rhonda got out and ran toward the entrance of the Emergency Room.

Mark was wheeled into the first available cubicle. When she wanted to follow him, she was directed to the admittance desk to fill out the necessary paperwork.

She'd just finished answering what seemed like a hundred pointless questions, when she was joined by Karl and Jen, along with the parents of the girl who had also been injured. Although Susan had been unrecognizable due to the amount of blood covering her body and face, Rhonda did recognize the parents.

"I'm so sorry Mr. and Mrs. Woodhall," she said, extending her hand.

Larry Woodhall composed himself and looked her directly in her eyes. "We were told your husband was also wounded, Detective Pohs. I've been advised he kept the other students safe. I only wish he'd arrived earlier and been able to save our Susan."

"I'm praying for her recovery. If you'll excuse me, I need to go back and see my husband."

Larry and his wife Nancy nodded their heads in tandem as though relieved to be left alone away from the scrutiny of the police. Not that they had any reason to fear the police but at a time like this no one wanted to be the center of attention.

She hurried back to where she left Mark, only to find the cubical empty.

"You didn't give us a chance to tell you," Jen said. "Mark was taken to surgery to take out the bullet. I tried to get your attention, but you were in such a hurry to get back here, you didn't notice me."

"Why didn't they notify me? They knew where I was."

"I told him we would let you know. Why don't we go down to the cafeteria?"

Karl gently took hold of her elbow and steered her away from the Emergency Department. "As I recall you didn't eat any of your lunch. I can tell you need something to eat and not necessarily the Ruben sandwich in the container in my car."

Rhonda nodded her agreement. She could feel the weakness starting to wash over her. Karl was right. She'd had a very light breakfast and since then only two cups of coffee and a half a glass of iced tea.

Once in the cafeteria, Jen told her to find them a table. As much as she wanted to pick out her own meal, she knew Jen would pick out something substantial. She knew she needed to sit down. Going through the line to pick out food would be too much for her, since her legs threatened to buckle at any minute.

Jen returned with a bowl of soup and a cup of yogurt. Also on the tray was a pager. Karl was right behind her with a roast beef sandwich and a side of mashed potatoes on his tray.

"Who do you think your feeding, The Hulk? I never eat this much for lunch."

"The sandwich and potatoes are for me," Karl replied. "I was driving, remember. I didn't get to eat my lunch either. I tried to get Jen to pick up a sandwich for you, but she insisted on soup and yogurt."

"She made a great choice. I don't know if I can even eat what's on my tray."

Rhonda tasted the chicken noodle soup and decided it compared nicely to any Mark made at home. As far as she was concerned, yogurt was yogurt. The more she ate the better she felt. The tears she'd shed while on the way to the hospital were now held at bay. She knew she needed to be strong for Mark.

She'd just finished eating when Karl's phone rang. Not wanting to eavesdrop, Rhonda continued her conversation with Jen.

"I'll be right there," Karl said, before pushing his chair away from the table. "I'm sorry, I need to get back to the office. They have the shooter in custody and want me to sit in on the interrogation. His name is Jason Munns. Does it mean anything to you?"

Rhonda thought for a minute. "I haven't heard Mark talk about him, but that doesn't mean much. It's a big school with a lot of students. Mark works mainly with the kids on the basketball and baseball teams. I'll be interested to hear what this kid has to say for himself."

"I'll make sure the interview is taped so you can hear it for yourself. When you're ready to leave the hospital, call me and I'll have a car sent over for you. I'd like to leave Jen here with you, but this case belongs to both of you. I think she should be in on the interview as well."

Karl no sooner left the cafeteria than the pager began to buzz. For a moment, she tried to remember where Jen told her to go.

"You must be waiting for word on someone in surgery," a woman she recognized as a nurse said. "A lot of people get confused when waiting for word about a loved one. I'm certain the doctor will meet you in the third floor waiting room. I'm not scheduled to get back to work for a while, so I'll take you."

Rhonda thanked the woman and followed her to the elevator. She looked at the woman's badge and was surprised to see the name Elizabeth Munns. Could this woman be related to the shooter? It was possible there was some connection, but since the name of the shooter wouldn't be released to the public, she would have no idea she could be related to the teenager who lost it and brought a gun to school that morning.

"Now I recognize you," Elizabeth said once they were in the elevator.

"I've seen your picture in the paper enough to know you're Detective Rhonda Pohs. I heard about the school shooting on TV this morning. I'm sorry about your husband. Thank goodness there weren't more casualties. My cousin, Jason, goes to school there. For a while, I was afraid he was the one who was shot, but then they said the victim was a girl."

"Why would you think Jason would have been a victim?" Rhonda asked, her interest now piqued.

"The poor kid is a number one nerd. The kids, especially the jocks, tease him mercilessly. He's a high functioning autistic and has a very high IQ. He gets good grades in all his classes, especially computer science. Socially it's a different matter. He has very few friends, but he also has a temper. The teasing bothers him a lot. I was worried one of the kids might have gotten sick of his outbursts and targeted him."

The information she'd just gleaned might be something she could use in the investigation of the school shooting, even though this wasn't her case, as Karl insinuated as much when he took Jen back to the office to sit in on the interrogation.

The elevator stopped at the third floor and Elizabeth escorted Rhonda to the waiting room before leaving to begin her scheduled shift.

Rhonda handed in the still buzzing disk at the desk. There, an older woman directed her to go to a small consultation room and have a seat to wait for the doctor. She wished Jen was with her. What if she melted into a puddle with the news of how his surgery went. This was Mark. He was her mainstay in her life. He had to be okay. She couldn't go on if anything unexpected happened to him.

She wasn't certain how long she would have to wait, but surprisingly the door behind her opened. She turned, expecting to see the doctor. Instead, Tyson stood in the doorway.

"What are you doing here? How did you know?"

"I was following the reports on TV when Karl called and said he had to leave you here all alone. I told him I'd come right away and make certain you would get home okay."

Before she could express her gratitude for his presence, the doctor entered the room.

"Mrs. Pohs, your husband came through surgery remarkably well. We do want to keep him overnight for observation. He was lucky the bullet was stopped by his collar bone. If that hadn't been the case, it's anyone's guess as to where it would have ended up. I was told he was shot at close range so the velocity of the bullet would have been accelerated. We were able to retrieve the bullet and sent it to the forensics department, although I'm told they have the shooter in custody and the gun. He's in recovery now and he'll be in a room in about half an hour. They'll be able to give you the room number at the desk. Do you have any questions for me?"

Rhonda gave her question a moment of thought before answering. "Will he be able to come home tomorrow?"

"We'll see how he does tonight, but things are looking good now. When he does go home, he'll be on painkillers. He'll be weak, but by next week he'll be able to go back to work. He won't be able to drive. I hear you are still unable to drive, so you'll have to find someone who can help you out."

"There is no problem with that," Tyson said. "I'll be able to take care of both of them until they are able to take care of themselves."

"Are you family?"

Tyson laughed. "I feel like we are. My mom and Mark's have been best friends since high school. We've become close since Mark and Rhonda moved here a few years ago. My job is flexible enough that I can take the time off to be with them."

"Tyson has been a godsend in more ways than one. I'm putting him up for fairy godfather of the year. We'll be in good hands."

Chapter Twelve

Karl stepped into the interrogation room, with Jen by his side. He couldn't believe the teenager who sat at the table with his parents was someone who, not only brought a gun to school with him, but shot a fellow student and a teacher before he was subdued.

"Our son has a lawyer," Mr. Munns declared as soon as Karl joined them.

"I understand," Karl replied. "How soon will your lawyer be here?"

"He said he'd be here by five."

Karl checked his watch. It surprised him to see it was four forty-five. Where had the day gone? He knew neither the kid nor his parents would say one word without their lawyer present.

Jen offered to get them some coffee. Karl knew he needed it and was surprised when the Munns family also took her up on her offer. Most of the people he interrogated said no immediately, afraid of the discarded cup being used for DNA collection.

At two minutes after five the lawyer arrived. "I would have been here earlier, but with traffic and all, it took longer than I thought it would. I'll be advising my client not to say anything to you."

"I'm sure you will, but you must understand there were almost two hundred witnesses as to what happened. I have no doubt of his guilt. What I want to know is why?"

The lawyer and Jason's parents huddled with Jason, while Karl waited for an answer.

"I've advised my client not to say anything. That said, Jason wants to make a statement."

Karl nodded toward the teenager.

"They are all such Goody Two-Shoes. They can't stand the fact I'm smarter than they are. I get teased a lot because they call me a computer nerd. They call me weird because I have autism and I don't socialize like they do. I'm not in the clique. I wanted them to see me as a person. If I bought the gun to school, I thought they would respect me for who I am, not who they think I am. I didn't want to hurt anyone."

"From the notes I was given by the officers on the scene, you were shouting something about Billy Roller. Did you have anything to do with that?"

"No. I didn't like the idea of having stoners at the school, but I didn't do anything to him."

"How can we be certain of that? It's just your word."

The lawyer tried to silence Jason, but he wrenched away.

"I can verify that Jason wasn't in town," Mr. Munns said. "Our son was so upset over the show being hosted by his school, we decided it was best if we went on a family vacation. We left Thursday night and drove to Phoenix to visit my parents. They have a winter condo there and they are planning to go back to Ohio soon. We thought it would be a good time to go for a visit. You can check things out with the school. He was excused on Friday."

"Is there anyone other than your parents who can vouch for you being in Phoenix on Saturday night?"

"We can. My parents and their next-door neighbors took us to a dinner show. We saw Joseph and the Technicolor Dream Coat at a local church. I have the ticket stubs at home."

Karl knew the story Mr. Munns told could easily be verified. Jason wasn't the person who killed Billy. He was a stressed-out teen with too much time on his hands.

"Let's get back to what happened today. You said you brought the gun to school to get respect from your fellow students. How is it that you shot Susan Woodward?"

"I was so upset about the Billy Roller show at the school, like my dad said, I refused to go. I kept telling people not to go to it, but they wouldn't listen to me. So, I talked to a friend who had a gun, and he gave it to me. I just wanted to show them I mattered too. I didn't mean for it to go off but when it did, I got scared. I was going to run out of the cafeteria. That's when I saw Mr. Pohs. I didn't know what happened until it went off again and I saw blood on Mr. Pohs' shirt. After that everything is a blur. No one will tell me if I killed anyone, I only wanted them to see me as something other than a computer nerd."

Karl contemplated Jason's confession. There had been so much in the news lately about students being bullied to the breaking point. Thankfully, he hadn't ever had to deal with it before now.

"The only thing I can tell you about Susan Woodhall and Mr. Phos is that they are still in surgery. I was called here from the hospital but at the time I had no information. I do have one question for you. Mr. Pohs has been receiving some threatening emails. Do you know anything about them?"

Jason's face went pale at the mention of the emails. "I did send them. I knew Mr. Pohs was responsible for bringing Billy Roller here so, I sent them to him. I only wanted to blow off steam. I didn't know any other way to do it."

"Can we take Jason home now?" Mrs. Munns asked.

Karl could tell the woman was stressed over what her son just confessed to. Any parent would be. "I'm afraid not. He's charged with a major crime. He'll be arraigned in the morning and that's when bail will be set."

Mrs. Munns became hysterical and hugged her son.

Karl read Jason his rights, even though he knew it had been done earlier at the school. The boy was in serious trouble. If either Susan or Mark were to die, the charge could be changed to murder.

"It's okay, Mom," Jason said. "By tomorrow things will be better."

Karl hoped Jason was right. As a precaution, he planned for the boy to have a cell by himself. He was far from a hardened criminal and if Karl read the kid right, he preferred being alone to being with others.

"Can you believe what we just heard?" Jen asked once Jason was taken away and the Munns left the room.

"Jason apparently lives in a different world than the rest of us. I don't think he had any idea that the gun would go off. No matter how smart he is academically, he's still stinted in social graces. A kid with Autism who is a computer nerd probably plays a lot of computer games. In them the characters don't die. I doubt he even knew the gun was loaded. It's a real grey area at this point."

~ * ~

Rhonda checked her watch repeatedly. The doctor told her Mark would be here in half an hour and now it was fifteen minutes past that. She knew she shouldn't be worried, but there was always concern when someone underwent surgery.

A commotion in the hallway alerted them to the fact Mark was being brought back to his room. One of the orderlies came in and asked them to leave until they were able to get him settled.

As Rhonda passed the bed in the hallway, she noticed how pale Mark looked. It was evident he wasn't completely with it because of the painkillers he was on. His left arm was being supported by a sling, meaning if the bullet had been a little lower, she might be planning a funeral rather than waiting to talk to her husband.

Tears prickled behind her eyelids, but she willed them not to fall. Tyson held her hand. Over the past few days, he had become her rock. The one stable thing to hold onto throughout all the drama that plagued her with this case.

A few minutes later, they were able to return to the room. Rhonda went immediately to the bed. She was relieved when Mark opened her eyes and recognized her.

"I can't believe you took a bullet," she said, trying to make light of the situation.

"I can't let you have all the fun," Mark replied, his words slurred. "I don't think I want to do anything like this again. Seeing that kid with a gun in his hand and hearing the shot when he discharged it, something went off in my head. I knew something had to be done and I was the only one in a position to do anything about it. I certainly didn't think he would turn around and shoot me, too. How is the girl he shot?"

"All we know is she is still in surgery. You don't know how badly you scared me. Promise me you won't do anything like that again."

Mark squeezed her hand, and it gave her the reassurance she needed. One never knew what was going to happen in life. It was no wonder he worried about her when she was on the job.

"How long are they going to keep me prisoner here?" Mark asked.

Rhonda could tell his strength was draining. "They said overnight. They'll know more in the morning."

"Do I have to guess why our unofficial bodyguard is here?"

Tyson grinned. "I doubt it. I heard about the shooting at the high school and contacted my boss. I'm your chauffeur until further notice, Being the great bodyguard I am, I'm planning to take Rhonda back to my loft tonight. It's a secure building and she won't be alone out at your house. Be prepared when you get home, because I'm going to be your houseguest. If you're anything like your wife I should have my hands full taking care of the two of you."

Tyson's comment broke the tension in the room. "I think that sounds like a great plan," Rhonda said.

The sound of someone entering the room caused Rhonda to turn and see Karl standing behind her. Her boss' presence reminded her she should have asked Mark what happened, but it wasn't her case. This was her husband. For a moment, she realized why physicians didn't treat their families. It was the same with cops. She was too personally involved to be rational where Mark was concerned.

"If you want me to tell you what went on at school, you're better off talking with the students who were there. It all happened so fast, I'm not sure I can tell you much."

Rhonda could hear Mark starting to slur his words.

"It won't be necessary. We've interviewed the shooter. His name is

Jason Munns and…"

"Did you say Jason Munns?" Rhonda interrupted, remembering her conversation with his cousin earlier in the day. "Did you know he's a high functioning autistic?"

"He told me that, but how did you know."

"His cousin is one of the nurses here. We happened to meet, and she said when she heard about the shooting, she was afraid someone at the school targeted him because he's different. He's not very social and has a temper. In other words, he's a loner in more ways than one."

"Instead, he was the one who targeted his classmates. Even though he admitted to everything, it was like he was playing a video game. When he saw Susan drop and bleed real blood, he panicked and tried to run away. That's when the gun went off again and he shot Mark. It was a semi-automatic so it's hard telling how many others he might have shot if he hadn't been stopped. He said he didn't want to hurt anyone, but he shot one of his classmates, to say nothing of you."

Rhonda took a deep breath. She'd been so concerned about Mark; she'd completely forgotten about Susan Woodhall and her parents. "Have you heard how Susan is doing?"

"I checked before I came up here," Karl replied. "She's out of surgery, but she's still in critical condition. I was told they couldn't give us any positive information for seventy-two hours. In other words, it's in God's hands. The bullet did a lot of damage to the internal organs. For tonight, Jason is in custody and awaiting arraignment tomorrow. He will be charged with two counts of attempted murder."

Rhonda could see Mark cringe at the charges against Jason Munns. It was possible he knew the young man who had caused so much damage, both mental and physical, at the school today.

"Do you know him, Mark?" Karl asked.

Rhonda wondered if this was the time to interrogate Mark. He was evidently exhausted from the surgery, to say nothing of the painkillers they had him on. Knowing Mark, he would do whatever he could to help with the investigation.

"It's more like I know of him. I was told I should talk to him about updating our website. I planned to visit him in the computer lab today. I don't understand any of this."

"In situations like this, no one does. I don't know enough about autism to decide one way or another. Considering the seriousness of the crime, I'm sure he will be sent to a juvenile facility until it's time for his trial. It doesn't seem right, but it wouldn't surprise me."

"That would be a shame. I certainly hope he's spared something like that." Mark commented.

Rhonda noticed the additional slurring of Mark's words and his cringe of pain as he became agitated over the thought of Jason being incarcerated.

"I think it's time for Tyson to take me back to his place. I need another painkiller. We'll be back in the morning."

After kissing Mark goodbye, she followed Karl and Tyson from the room. Once they were out in the hall, she turned to Karl. "Is the Munns kid good for Bill's murder?"

Karl shook his head. "He was in Phoenix that weekend with his parents and grandparents. I don't know what's going to happen to him. He's a nerd who is socially handicapped, be it due to overly protective parents or his autism, I can't say."

"It sounds like you're talking about a puppy," Tyson quipped. "They need to be socialized. I didn't think it was the same with kids."

"That's a good comparison, but I have a feeling his parents shielded him. It would have stinted his social growth."

"What does that have to do with Bill's murder?" Rhonda inquired.

"He was upset about Billy playing at his high school. He said he tried to talk to people about not going to the show, but no one would listen to him. He knew Mark was the one who brought the show to the school, so he started sending the threatening emails to him. To be truthful, I have a feeling the kid's lawyer will be using an insanity plea. The only thing we can hope is for the girl to pull through, which at this point is debatable. If she dies, everything changes. He'll be charged with first degree murder. At his age he can be tried as an adult and end up in the prison system for the rest of his natural life."

Rhonda didn't want to hear about the what if's, the exhaustion of the day's events were closing in on her. With it came the headache that had been her constant companion since the events in Idaho changed her life.

On one hand she wanted the kid responsible for Mark being in the hospital to remain in custody. She also wanted Susan Woodhall to pull through. On the other hand, she felt sorry for Jason and wanted nothing more than for this case to be over and done with. More than anything else, she wanted to get back to work and figure out who killed Bill.

"Take her home, Tyson," Karl said. "I'm sure she has the painkillers in her purse. They should be enough to knock her out for tonight. I'll touch base with you in the morning, but right now Mark needs her more than I do."

"That's not fair and you know it," Rhonda protested. "Once I get Mark home and settled, I'll have Tyson bring me to work. I promise I won't leave my desk. I still have hundreds of pictures to go through. I want this case solved and I want it sooner rather than later."

"You'll do as you're told. If you want to go over those photos, I'll have them transferred to your laptop and send it, as well as Jen, over to your place to work with you. Since Tyson is content to be babysitting you and Mark, I think he can handle one more charge."

Chapter Thirteen

Rhonda spent an uneasy night in Tyson's loft. Even though he insisted she take his bed while he crashed on the couch, she was plagued with dreams of Mark being shot after enduring the uncertainty of the threatening emails.

The night before, they'd stopped by the house, while she picked up a change of clothes she'd need for the morning, along with personal hygiene products she didn't expect to need. With all the stress she'd been under lately, it was possible her body's physical clock could be out of sync and she wanted to be prepared.

As soon as they ". When we're finished, we'll go over to your place and the two of you can look at all the pictures you want."

~ * ~

Mark looked much better when they picked him up. It wasn't surprising to find the press waiting for them when they left the hospital.

"Mr. Pohs, we were told you were the one who stopped the shooter at the school yesterday. How does it feel to be a hero?"

Before Tyson could intervene, Mark answered their question. "I don't consider myself a hero, I only did what I felt was necessary to keep more students from being injured."

"With the shooter in custody, are you hoping for him to get the maximum sentence?"

"How long before you're going to be able to go back to school?"

Mark looked at Rhonda and didn't answer until she nodded. Rather than step on any legal toes, he needed her approval. This was one question he could comment on. "I plan to visit there tomorrow and go back to work a week from Monday. I've been off since the murder of Billy Roller. This time it's my doctor who says I need time to recuperate."

Other reporters clamored with their microphones at the ready as Tyson pulled up in his vehicle. Once he got out, he held up his hand for silence. "I'm sure you don't want to exhaust Mr. Pohs before he can get home. He wants to thank you for your concern and asks you to respect his privacy."

Tyson helped Mark get into the front seat, while Rhonda got into the back. She could almost visualize the pictures that would grace the front pages of the papers either later tonight or tomorrow morning.

"Has there been any word on Susan's condition?" Mark asked, as they drove toward the restaurant.

"I was listening to the news on TV this morning," Tyson replied, "they say she's still in ICU but has been upgraded from critical to fair condition. It sounds like she'll make it."

Rhonda prayed the girl would make a complete recovery but knew the trauma of what happened would stay with her for the rest of her life. She'd been told there was a lot of damage to Susan's internal organs and it was possible she'd never have children.

They pulled into the parking lot of the restaurant, and she smiled to see Karl's vehicle there. She was certain Karl and Jen were waiting for them to arrive.

Inside the restaurant, they were taken to a table for five. Jen looked rested, while Karl appeared to be distressed.

"It's good to see you out of that bed," Karl said, getting to his feet and shaking Mark's hand. "We ordered coffee all around. You guys drink coffee, don't you?"

Mark winked at Rhonda. "Being married to Rhonda, I've learned to live on coffee when she's on a case. To be truthful I got addicted to it when I was in college and pulling those all-nighters."

"I'm guilty of the same addiction," Tyson said, once he seated himself at the table.

"Do you have anything more to tell us about Jason Munns?" Rhonda asked after they placed their orders.

"He was arraigned this morning; he's charged with two counts of attempted murder. His parents wanted him to be released into their custody, but the judge ordered bail of a million dollars and requested he be taken to a psychiatric facility for evaluation."

"That's a shame. Although I never met him in person, all his teachers spoke highly of him. Since I deal mainly with sports, our paths never crossed. He borders on genius status but is lacking socially. It's always hard to tell when someone like him has autism. I'm still in shock over that one."

"For now, he's in safe hands. Jen has the laptops in the trunk of my car. When we finish eating, we'll transfer them to Tyson's vehicle and the two of you can get to work."

As much as Rhonda wished she could be in the office, she also knew she needed to be with Mark. With no leads in the Billy Roller case, as everyone called it, she knew she could work from home as easily as from the office.

~ * ~

After they arrived at the house, Mark went into the bedroom for a nap while Tyson drove to the closest grocery store to restock the kitchen. Until the excitement died down, they all agreed it would be best if they didn't go out to eat to avoid the press, Tyson also suggested they get something delivered for dinner.

It seemed strange to be in the house, especially having Tyson and Jen with them. Once things quieted down, Rhonda and Jen set up their laptops and took seats side by side at the dining room table.

The first document she looked at was Bill's most recent will. There were gifts to be given to various charities as well as a large sum to his parents. Other than those bequeaths, the bulk of his estate, well over ten million dollars, was to go to Connie and the baby. The date he signed the will was a day and a half before his murder, as well as a day before the wedding.

Everything was as she suspected it to be.

"Connie is going to be a very wealthy woman," Jen said, breaking their silence.

"It looks that way. From what Rusty told me, they both had wills drawn up on the same day by the same attorney, I'm sure she knew exactly what this will said."

"It does seem funny these wills were written on one day, they were married the next and he was killed that night, I don't have a good feeling about this; it feels like a bad omen."

The next document was the original will. In it, everything other than the special bequeaths was left to his parents.

Rhonda set the wills aside and started scanning the pictures on the computer, comparing them to the picture she'd had the IT department print out for her the day before. As she did, she wondered how it could have been only yesterday when she started looking at the pictures. So much had happened, it felt as though a week had passed, rather than one day.

"I found a picture of him," Jen declared, bringing Rhonda back to the task at hand.

Jen turned her computer so Rhonda could see what she was talking about. There was no doubt the picture of the same young man who photo bombed the wedding picture was displayed on the screen. He was in the background, but he was there all the same.

By the time Mark got up from his nap. They'd found five more pictures of the Mystery man. Like the other photos, he was always in the background and never photographed with anyone but Connie and Bill. It was easy to tell they were taken at several venues when Bill and the band appeared. Each time a picture was found, Rhonda sent it to Mark's wireless printer and made two copies. That way, both she and Jen would have one for their files. Tomorrow when they returned to the office, they could have more copies made for anyone else who might be working on the case.

"Any progress?" Mark asked when he joined them in the dining room.

"We've found six pictures of the mystery man, He's never in the center of any pictures, but he's always either photo bombing Bill and Connie or in the crowd. It's almost like he was one of the groupies following the band from show to show or he was a stalker. He's always there but no one knows who he is."

Mark sat across the table from Rhonda and Jen and looked through the stack of printed pictures, each showing the man in different locations. "Interesting," he remarked. "I hope you'll be able to find out who this guy is."

"Did you find more pictures?" Tyson asked as he came in from the garage carrying the groceries.

"They sure did. I think he might be the key to their whole investigation, I've learned to never underestimate anything where my wife and her partner are concerned."

Everyone enjoyed a laugh that seemed to break the tension in the room.

~ * ~

Later that afternoon, after Karl stopped by to pick up Jen, Tyson called to have dinner delivered. Had it been Rhonda placing the order, she would have opted for pizza, but Tyson ordered from an app on his phone.

"What are we having for dinner tonight?" she asked when Tyson put away his phone.

"If I told you, you'd know as much as I do. I want this to be a surprise. You do know how to use chopsticks, don't you?"

Rhonda shook her head, "I never learned the art."

"In that case, you'd better get out some silverware."

"Ah Chinese," Mark commented. "I can taste it already."

"Not so fast, buddy. I didn't say a word about Chinese."

The doorbell rang and Tyson went to answer it. As soon as the delivery person handed him the food he was gone. It was evident Tyson had paid for everything when he placed the order.

Rhonda could smell the delectable aroma coming from the carry-out containers Tyson was setting on the counter.

"I hope you like Fried Rice and Chicken Satay. I love Thai food," Tyson said. "My favorite restaurant for it is Le Thai."

"It smells absolutely delicious," Rhonda admitted.

She watched as Tyson unwrapped his chopsticks while she and Mark used their silverware to dig into the delectable dishes before them. She wished she'd learned how to use those ancient eating utensils. Watching someone use them with such precision was like observing an artist at work.

"What do you think?" Tyson asked once they finished eating.

"I never thought I'd like Thai food because of the spice, but this was fantastic," Mark admitted.

"If we were having this at my place, I would be serving some good wine with it. Of course, since the two of you are still on painkillers, I wouldn't think of giving you alcohol."

Rhonda laughed at how serious he sounded. "I'm glad you're the one taking care of us. You know how to make us laugh at ourselves. It's too bad we can't keep you here to order fantastic meals for us."

Mark pretended to pout at her comment, "I thought you liked my fantastic gourmet cooking."

"You know I do, my love."

Once everything was cleaned up, they sat down to watch TV. They were surprised to find a rerun of Until Someone Gets Hurt, Tyson's documentary for Investigation /discovery. They'd watched it when it first came out and knew the story from reading Tyson's book by the same title. Watching it tonight with Tyson allowed Rhona to see, firsthand, the emotions behind the events he'd lived through. The drama alone was enough to bring tears to Rhonda's eyes.

The program ended and Rhonda was getting ready for bed when she received a call from Karl.

"I think you should turn on the news."

"Why? What's up?"

"While the Munns family was raising the bail money, Jason was beat up in the commons area of the hospital. The fight broke out so fast none of the orderlies could get there in time. One of the patients had a homemade knife and he used it. Jason isn't dead, but he's in the same hospital as Susan. From the reports, they're both fighting for their lives."

"I thought Susan was doing much better."

"She was, but she took a bad turn late this afternoon. I just talked to the doctors and it's not looking good at this point.

"From what I heard from the hospital, the patient who stabbed Jason said it was one thing for a hardened criminal to kill someone, but for a kid to go to school with a gun was just wrong You know all the coverage they've had on the shooting; a lot of people are up in arms about this. Add to that the reason these patients are at the hospital and you're asking for trouble. I was hoping they would send Jason to a juvenile facility for evaluation."

Rhonda took a deep breath before posing the question that was foremost on her mind, "Is there anything I can do?"

"Like I told you before, this isn't your case. Let the investigating officers do their work. You're too closely related to it. How is Mark doing?"

"He's better tonight but he's more than ready for bed. I don't think he's used many of the painkillers today, so when he took one tonight, it knocked him right out."

"That's good. Then you and Jen will be back on the job tomorrow. Do you want me to send a car for you?"

"That won't be necessary. Tyson said he'd drive me to work before he takes Mark over to the high school. He feels like he should be there to reassure the kids."

"Just so he's aware of it, the area around the school is filled with flowers and teddy bears, I drove out that way after we had breakfast this morning, and was shocked by the sheer amount of flowers there were in that memorial."

Tears were flowing down Rhonda's cheeks when the call ended. Although she thought Mark was asleep, she was surprised to see him enter the living room.

"What's wrong?" Mark asked.

She wanted to wait until morning to tell Mark, but considering he was awake, she knew she had to fill him in now. "Susan has taken a turn for the worst, and they don't know if she's going to make it. In another twist, Jason was stabbed in a fight at the hospital. The ironic thing is they're in the same hospital and neither of them is expected to make it. What a terrible waste, all because a kid was bullied at school."

Mark crossed the few feet that separated them and sat beside her on the couch, hugging her with his good arm. "Another sad thing is at the last teacher's meeting we had; we discussed the problem of bullying. It was the consensus that we didn't have a problem with it. I have a feeling we will be revisiting this discussion and putting some anti-bullying policy in effect. I can't believe because of these terrible things kids do to one another, two students are fighting for their lives tonight."

"Don't forget the damage done to you," Tyson reminded him.

"That's minor. I'll recover. What if one or both kids don't make it? If something happened to me, it would be tragic for Rhonda, but I've lived a good life and have no regrets. Neither of these kids have had a chance to live. Susan is one of the cheerleaders for the basketball team and is extremely popular. I also know Jason has an exceptional mind and, from what I'm told, he was going to be offered a scholarship to a good college for computer studies. How does a kid do something like this when he's only a sophomore, and in one moment throws everything away?"

Rhonda ached for Mark's pain. She knew he loved every kid in the school even if they weren't in any of the sports programs he coached. He was the kind of role model kids looked up to and respected.

Chapter Fourteen

Rhonda and Mark were awake long before the alarm went off. They'd each spent a restless night, but not because of being uncomfortable or in pain. Many times during the night, they realized their partner would be away and they talked about the phone call from Karl just before they went to bed.

"I wish I could go to the school with you this morning," Rhonda said.

"I do too, but you have a job to do. I'm just making an appearance to assure the kids I'm okay."

"I guess neither of us is going to get any more sleep. I'm going to take a shower and get ready for work."

By the time Rhonda returned to the bedroom, Mark was up. She could tell he'd used the guest bathroom to clean up and shave.

"I thought I could get dressed on my own, but can you help me get on my shirt and sweats?"

Rhonda smiled. She could imagine how hard he would struggle, not only with putting on a shirt, but buttoning and zipping up his slacks. "Of course, I will."

After searching his closet, she pulled out a pair of sweatpants along with a zip up shirt she knew ne never liked, but it would be easy for him to put on. Being knit, it wouldn't be as restricting as a dress shirt or even a pullover.

By the time they finished dressing, they could smell something delicious being prepared in the kitchen. Rhonda smiled when she saw Tyson standing at the stove, making omelets while bacon sizzled in another frying pan.

"I didn't know you could cook," Mark teased.

"It's one of my many talents. Being a bachelor, I have to know how to fend for myself when I don't feel like going out. Mom taught me the basics and I've added to my skills over the years. I can grill a great steak, if I need to, I also make a mean omelet. Hope you like vegetarian omelets with Swiss cheese."

Rhonda's mouth watered at the thought of having one of her favorite breakfasts. Usually, the two of them were in such a hurry they either fried up a couple of eggs or dined on cold cereal and toast.

As they were leaving, Rhonda's phone rang. "Pohs here."

"Good morning, Rhonda, this is Karl. There's been a change of plans. I'm picking up Jen and we'll meet you at Mark's school."

"What's going on?"

"Maybe nothing but we got a call reporting a crowd gathering there, staging a demonstration."

"Have you had any word from the hospital?"

There was a long silence on the other end of the line. "Susan Woodhall died this morning at about three."

Rhonda could feel her shoulders slump at the news. Susan was dead and if Jason survived, he would be charged with first degree murder. What a terrible end to two promising young students.

After explaining everything to Mark and Tyson, they made the ten-minute drive from the house to the school. At the time they purchased the house, she questioned the proximity to the school. Now she was glad they didn't have a long drive.

As soon as they turned onto the road where the school was situated, they could see cars and vans lining both sides of the road, meaning parking was at a premium. Rather than jockey for a parking space, Tyson pulled up in front of the school. After Rhonda and Mark exited the vehicle, he pulled away to find a spot to park before joining them.

Rhonda once again showed her badge to gain the school grounds. She was shocked to see the amount of flowers and banners. One banner hanging over the doorway to the doorway to the school read: WE LOVE YOU COACH POHS.

Beside her, she could feel Mark tense. "I-I didn't expect this," he said, his voice expressing the emotions he was trying to keep in check.

She wanted to reply, but the chants from the crowd drowned out her words.

"Jason Munns deserves the death penalty," were the words she could make out from the demonstrators.

As soon as someone saw them coming toward the building the chant changed to. "Coach Pohs, Coach Pohs, he's our man. If he can't save us, no one can."

"It sounds like you're a real hero to these kids," she shouted to be heard over the yelling of the students and parents.

To her surprise, Mark lifted is free hand for silence. The shouts died down and a hushed quiet surrounded the school.

"Coach Pohs," a young girl called as she rushed to his side, tears streaking down her face. "Have you heard? That bastard killed Susan. She died this morning. What's going to happen to Jason now?"

Rhonda could see the emotions playing out on Mark's face as the girl spoke, asking questions without answers.

"We appreciate your praise of my husband but what are you planning to do with this demonstration?"

"We just want to see justice done. Jason is a murderer," another student shouted.

Mark seemed to regain his composure. "I think it's best if everyone goes into the gym. There are more police officers arriving shortly. We need to set the record straight about what happened here on Monday. There is a student dead, but it could have been far worse. Unfortunately, it wasn't just Jason who pulled the trigger."

There were murmurs from the students and parents who turned to go into the school. The process of clearing the crowd of demonstrators was completely orderly. It was as though they were all thinking about what Mark said. To be truthful, Rhonda was wondering what he meant as well.

The last of the students and parents entered the room, just as Tyson arrived, followed by Karl and Jen. Along with them was a reporter.

"I heard what you said out there, Coach Pohs," the reporter began, "What did you mean it wasn't just Jason who pulled the trigger? He was the one who brought the gun to school."

"Between Sheriff Brannigan, my wife, her partner and myself, I think we can explain everything once everyone is in the gym. You're free to join us."

Rhonda followed Mark into the school and down the hall toward the gym. On the way they passed the auditorium, where just days ago Billy Roller was scheduled to put on a show but because of his murder, he was absent. From what Karl told her, the show was the catalyst for, not only the murder, but the death of a young girl, the stabbing of a teenage boy, along with the wounding of her husband.

Before entering the gym, Mark stopped to talk to the principal of the school. Rhonda couldn't hear what was being said, but the older man nodded his head and hurried off.

When they entered the gym, students and parents filled the pull-out bleachers on both sides of the room. The overflow sat on the floor. A buzz of conversation filled the room, but as soon as they entered it became eerily silent.

Rhonda saw several teachers rushing around to set up a makeshift podium with a microphone.

"What are you going to tell them?" Rhonda asked.

"The truth. There's nothing wrong with that, is there?"

"Not at all."

Mark crossed the room and stood at the podium. "On Monday, a terrible thing happened at this school. A fine young student is dead, I was wounded, and Jason Munns said he committed the crime. It's an open and shut case, or is it? How many of you knew who Jason was? Not just a nodding acquaintance but knew the real Jason."

Mark paused while a few of the students raised their hands.

"How many of you had classes with him and made fun of him because you thought he was a nerd?"

Several more hands went up.

"Like so many school shootings, this one was the result of bullying. Jason was a computer genius. He also has autism. He's high functioning with a high IQ, but socially he isn't on the same level as other kids his age. He thinks school should be a place for education and he couldn't understand all the hype about the Billy Roller concert. His parents took him out of town the weekend of the concert. Jason said he tried to talk to several of you about his concerns, but no one would listen to him. In the end, he snapped. He didn't want to be an outcast any longer. He thought if he brought a gun to school and threatened people, he would be someone to be reckoned with. Unfortunately, the gun went off, not once but twice. Bullying is a terrible thing. It went on when I was in high school, and it will continue long after I'm no longer coaching and you're no longer students. That is if you don't draw a line in the sand and decide to no longer tolerate such behavior from yourselves and your friends. Get to know your fellow classmates before you criticize them. You might be surprised with what you learn, or maybe even make a new friend in the process."

"What's going to happen to Jason?" one of the students who raised his hand as a friend of Jason's called out.

"It's hard to say," Karl said. "Right now, he's in the hospital and is fighting for his life. During the short time he was at the psychiatric hospital, he was stabbed. If he lives, he will be charged with first degree murder and attempted murder. If he dies, there is no one else to blame, or maybe there is. Like Coach Pohs just said, it's possible you will all conclude that bullying caused Jason to snap."

Another student got to his feet. Rhonda immediately recognized him as one of the stars of the basketball team.

"I know Jason, too. We were next door neighbors back when we were in elementary school. When Jason found out my parents were sending me here to school, he got his parents to send him here as well, I think he thought we were going to hang out together, but I made the basketball team. I also made new friends and Jason didn't fit in our circle. I guess I'm as much to blame as anyone, I didn't see it as bullying, we just grew apart."

After the young man sat down, a young girl stood up. "Jason asked me to homecoming with him last year, but I already had a date, He didn't take it well at all. I told him I was sorry, but he told me I'd regret what I did to him."

Rhonda searched the faces of the students. She could tell they were all thinking of how they'd treated, not only Jason, but other kids like him over the years. "If anyone would like to talk, my partner Detective Sims and I, along with our boss, Sheriff Brannigan, will be here to answer your questions and talk to you about bullying and how it affects not just the person being bullied. It also affects everyone else you know. It's like monkey see monkey do. If it's okay for my friend to bully someone, it's the same for me. Like the ripples in a pond, it moves out and soon it's a common practice. Like an epidemic, it spreads like wildfire. If your parents aren't already here, and you want them with you, don't hesitate to call them."

She turned back to Karl to see he, along with Jen, were already on their phones. Jen was calling other people to come in to help with the counseling sessions. The expression on Karl's face told her he wasn't soliciting help.

Karl hung up the phone. "Jason had a blood clot that went to his heart. They told his parents he was brain dead. An hour ago, they made the agonizing decision to take him off life support. He passed away after five minutes."

"We need to tell the kids," Rhonda said, with tears running down her cheeks.

~ * ~

By the end of the day, Rhonda felt as though she'd spoken to every sector of students at the high school. The kids who came to see her were sports stars, cheerleaders, computer nerds and common ordinary students who fell into all the groups in between.

She felt sorry for every one of them. Some were friends of Jason's who told of being bullied by the jocks and top students. Others were honor students who didn't realize that by not socializing with the nerds they were fueling the insecurity of their classmates.

After the last of the students left her station in the gym, Rhonda stood up and massaged her neck. She was exhausted and the headache she'd become used to returned with a vengeance. Across the room she saw Mark and Jen. It was evident they were also fatigued.

Throughout the day, Tyson worked with the teachers, organizing appointments for the students who wanted to talk.

Even though Rhonda felt as though she'd counseled every one of the kids, she knew she'd seen only a minute portion of them. Around the room, police officers, clergy, teachers and social workers all took their turns counseling the students who were reeling from the three tragic deaths that had plagued their school in the past few weeks.

"It's been a long day," Karl said as he approached her table. "What do you say we call it a day and go out for something to eat?"

"My thoughts exactly," Tyson agreed. "I have a friend who runs a restaurant not far from here. He called me and said he'd heard about what was going on. He told me he has a private dining room and I'm to invite anyone who wants to join us for dinner, on him. I took the liberty of calling Jen's boyfriend, Paul, and he will be meeting us there."

Karl smiled at Tyson's invitation. "Guess it pays to have friends in high places. I'm grateful for the invitation. Sometimes I wonder if Joe Public appreciates what we do and why we do it. You've renewed my faith in my fellow man."

Rhonda watched as Karl pumped Tyson's hand and slapped him on the back.

She vaguely remembered the ham sandwich the cafeteria brought up at noon along with a piece of fruit and carrot sticks with ranch dip. It was only about five hours ago and yet it seemed as though it had been days since she had anything to eat.

"You look beat," Mark said as he joined her. "I know how you feel. This certainly wasn't what I was planning on when I said I wanted to come back to the school for a visit today."

"I hear you there. How do you handle all these kids? Give me a murder investigation to a day like this anytime."

Mark laughed at her joke, not knowing she meant it from the bottom of her heart. She certainly didn't do well with teenagers.

~ * ~

Several of the people who ran the counseling sessions throughout the day joined them at the restaurant. Teachers sat in groups talking quietly about the day's events, while the clergy sat with others of their calling.

At a table for six, Rhonda along with Mark, Jen, Paul, Tyson and Karl talked in hushed tones about the deaths of both Susan and Jason.

"I hope I never have another day like this one," Jen confessed as they were being served their meals.

"Well said," Rhonda agreed. "With all the excitement we didn't get to talk about what we found out yesterday. Remember I told you about the man who photobombed Bill and Connie at the wedding?"

Karl nodded. "What about him?"

"We found six other pictures of him. What I find odd is that none of the band members could identify him other than they thought he was just another groupie. We also read Bill's will. I still find it strange it was filed the day before the wedding and names Connie as the main recipient of the funds from his estate. There were other bequeaths but most of his estate, as well as future royalties for his albums and other sales, all go to Connie. That young lady is going to be a multimillionaire."

Karl looked at her skeptically. "Do you think she had something to do with the murder?"

"I don't know. What I do know is she stood dry-eyed throughout the entire memorial services. At the time I thought it was a strange reaction. I questioned if she knew about the will, then I saw a second will. It was Connie's, signed and dated at the same time as Bill's. He knew what was in her will, just as she knew what was in his. I don't think she's as innocent as she makes out to be. I just don't have enough evidence to prove it."

Chapter Fifteen

The next morning, Rhonda returned to the office. With the chaos of yesterday behind her, she was glad to return to some semblance of normalcy. Reaching into her briefcase, she pulled out the copies of the pictures she printed off two days ago.

"Is there any way we can use facial recognition software to put a name to a face?" she asked as she entered the IT department.

"We can try," one of the techs said. "What do you have for us?"

Rhonda handed over the six pictures with the same man in the background. "I want to know who this man is."

"I don't know if we'll come up with anything. We will be checking it against driver's licenses from Nevada and California."

"Check Wisconsin and Illinois as well, I want to be sure to cover all of our bases."

She left the techs to do their jobs and went up to her office. At this point she wasn't feeling optimistic, but hopefully, the facial recognition software would give her a name for the man who always seemed to show up in Bill's pictures, even though no one in the band knew him.

"Any luck with IT? Jen asked when Rhonda entered the office."

"I can only hope. They're trying to match the picture to driver's license pictures. They were only going to check California and Nevada. For some reason, I didn't think that was enough. I asked them to check Wisconsin and Illinois. I was certain they thought I was out of my mind, but when I explained Bill came from Wisconsin and Connie from Illinois. They understood where I was coming from."

"I've been busy too. I checked the emails this morning and Rusty sent us some more pictures he found, I've found at least four more pictures of Mr. X. I hope the IT department can make an identification."

Rhonda studied the pictures on the screen of Jen's laptop. She had to look at them closely but when she did, the man was there in the background. It was hard to believe Rusty and the rest of the members of Bill's company had no idea who he was.

Rhonda's phone rang and she checked the caller ID to see if she recognized the number. When she did, she saw the call came from Phil Mason.

"Good morning, Phil," she said, omitting her usual greeting of 'Pohs here'.

"Do I have the right number? Is this my old partner who is always all business?" he teased.

"You know it is. I saw it was you who was calling. What's up?"

"I heard what went on out there Monday. I was concerned about Mark, as well as you. I also saw what went on at the school yesterday. It looks like you've got a nasty one on your hands."

"We do. We all spent all day yesterday in counseling sessions with the kids. When we got there, they were treating Mark like a hero. When he pointed out the dangers of bullying, I think the kids were all shocked to be shown the part they played in the murder of Susan Woodall."

"I saw where the girl died. I have a problem when it's a kid that gets killed. I also heard the shooter got beat up at the psychiatric facility. Have you heard anything about his condition?"

"I'm surprised it hasn't made the news yet. Jason died yesterday afternoon. At least someone else is going to have to investigate the facility on this one. I don't need any more murders at this point in the game. Talk about a waste of a young life. Jason was a high functioning autistic. He was highly intelligent and destined for great things in the computer world."

"I was hoping you'd tell me he was going to make it and get the help he needs. I've been reading about school shooters. The ones who don't kill themselves at the scene, are living quiet lives in prison."

"Let's change the subject. How long will it be before Mark can go back to work?"

Rhonda considered her answer. "The doctors say not for two weeks, but he's chomping at the bit. You know how he is. It's softball season and he wants to be with his team. We'll see how long Tyson and the doctors can contain him."

"Tyson?"

"He's taken some time off work to play nursemaid, I don't think Mark will stand for it much longer. He doesn't like to be down for too long."

"Have you gotten any leads about the photo bomber guy?"

"We thought he might be the one sending Mark the emails, but Jason confessed to being the one who did it. We've found several more photos of Mr. X and I turned everything over to the IT department. Hopefully, they will be able to find him through facial recognition from driver's license photos."

"Have you gotten any leads about the photo bomb guy?"

Rhonda explained about the other photos they'd found of Mr. X and how she'd turned it over to the IT department for further evaluation. By the time they ended their call, she still had no more information than she did earlier in the morning.

"I heard you talking to Phil Mason," Karl said as he entered her office. "I decided not to interrupt. We got word this morning from Idaho. They're transferring Axton to us tomorrow. They think he's stable enough to bring him in on a private plane. That said, I'm sending two of the members of our swat team meet their flight and bring him in."

The thought of someone else bringing Axton into the jail grated on Rhonda. "This is my case. Don't you think Jen and I should bring him in?"

"Hardly. I saw what he did to the two of you in Idaho. I don't want a repeat performance. It's safer with the swat team doing it. They are better trained to handle situations like this."

Both Rhonda and Jen agreed with his argument. The beating the two of them took in Idaho was still fresh in their minds.

~ * ~

It was almost time for Rhonda to go home when she received a call from the IT department. They'd found a match to the photo from four different states. From California, the name on the license was Jeffrey Adams. From Nevada, it was Anson Wallace, from Wisconsin it was Andrew Paulson, and from Illinois, Wade Johnson.

"How can someone have four licenses from four states with different names on each one?" Jen asked.

"People lie all the time to disguise who they are. It could be anything from witness protection to someone like Bill, to something more ominous. Whoever this guy is, I have a feeling he more than likely falls into the third category."

Before leaving for the day, Rhonda called Rusty, asking him if any of the names rang a bell with him. Since he didn't recognize any of them, she decided tomorrow she would broaden their search to include the rest of the country. If the man had four licenses, it was entirely possible he could have several more.

~ * ~

Tyson was waiting for her in the parking lot. "You look like you have a lot on your mind," he said. "Is there anything I can do to help?"

Rhonda shook her head.

"I have a lead, but the guy I'm looking at doesn't seem to exist. It's like he's a ghost in the wind."

"Sounds mysterious."

"It is, but it's my mystery. Guess that's why I make the big bucks."

Tyson laughed at her statement, but she knew he understood her position.

"I've got good and bad news. The good news is I took Mark to the doctor this morning. The doctor cleared him to go back to work. He still can't drive, but he assures me he can get a ride from one of the other teachers. Considering the person who sent the emails is no longer a problem, he no longer needs a bodyguard. The bad news is my boss called and he wants me to fly out tomorrow morning to put out some fires. I feel badly about leaving you and Mark without a driver."

Rhonda took a moment to digest the implications of what Tyson just told her. Without Tyson staying at the house the entire dynamic of their home life was about to change.

"I understand. I won't have a problem with it, since I haven't taken any pain killers for the past two days. I should be cleared to drive. As for Mark, it sounds as though he's solved the problem of transportation, and the doctor has cleared him to be back to work. We've imposed on you for too long. You know we appreciate everything you've done for us since this nightmare began."

"As soon as I put out the fires, I'll be back, and you know you can call on me."

"You're so sweet. I wish you could solve this one for me."

During the remainder of the ride home, they engaged in small talk. Once they pulled up, Tyson told her to go in and change her clothes. "Why do I need to change my clothes?"

"This is my last night with you and Mark. I want you to be my guests for dinner."

"We've been your guests more than is necessary. Why don't you let me cook something for you."

"Thanks, but no thanks. I've heard all about your cooking and I'd rather go out. I've heard about a new restaurant I've been anxious to try, I think you'll like it too. To be truthful, Mark gave me the same argument, but he still has trouble working in the kitchen one-handed. Letting me take you out is thanks enough."

Rhonda smiled and assessed Tyson's attire. He was dressed in designer jeans and an expensive polo shirt. She knew she could go casual and still fit in perfectly for an evening out with friends.

She also marveled at the man they both called friend. He was the best friend they ever encountered. She enjoyed the friendship of people in Wisconsin, but there were none who would put their life on hold during this crisis. No one who would have pulled strings to have Mark flown to Idaho when she sustained her injuries or gone with them to a funeral halfway across the country. She knew they wanted to find a way to repay him for all his generosity, but what could they give the man who had everything? If he wanted it, he would go out and buy it for himself.

Mark waited for them in the living room. He dressed in a like manner to Tyson. She noticed he looked tired but decided not to say anything about her misgivings concerning his going back to school in the morning. She knew that had to have such terrible memories for him, she worried about the consequences of it. "Let me guess, Tyson talked you into going out to dinner tonight," Mark said, after he gave her a kiss on the cheek.

"He can be very persuasive. Give me a few minutes to get a shower and change. I need to get the stink of the station off me."

Both men nodded their agreement as she headed for the master bathroom.

~ * ~

Once they got back to the house after dinner, Rhonda realized how much she would miss Tyson. He had been a permanent fixture in their lives since the murder of Bill occurred. He was indeed a good friend, but she knew he had his own life to live.

Rhonda and Mark were settling down for the night when she asked the question weighing on her mind. "How do you feel about going back to school tomorrow? Are you anxious?"

"No more so than the kids. I gave them quite a wake-up call at that assembly the other day. They are either going to hate me or thank me for pointing out the consequences of bullying. I talked to several of the other teachers. Although they are dealing with the deaths of two of their classmates it's a mixed bag on the subject of bullying.

"At this point I'm more worried about you. I could tell something was bothering you at dinner tonight. Is there anything I can do to help you out?"

"I wish I could say there was, but I'm afraid this is one tough nut to crack and I'm the one who has to crack it."

114

"I know you can't tell me much, but do you have a lead?"

"We do have a lead, but that's all it is. I don't know how we will be able to track it down. For now, it is just a face in the crowd. I can't even put a name to the face. It's frustrating."

"It will all fall in place. It always does. The problem is, I don't think this one's going to be solved in a timely manner, I know you want it to be in the books rather than a cold case, but sometimes what we want and what we get are two entirely different things."

Chapter Sixteen
Five Months Later

"Is there anything new on the Billy Roller case?" Karl asked when he entered Rhonda's office.

She allowed an exasperated sigh to pass her lips. Karl knew as well as she did there were no new leads. He asked the same question every morning knowing he would receive the same answer. The mystery man from the photos remained a mystery.

The IT department found six more hits from the photo recognition program, bringing them six more driver's licenses from six different states and as many different names. Each state corresponded with the venues where Billy and the Rollers held their concerts.

"Nothing new, Karl. You know there have been more than one other cases that have been easier to solve. This one is too close. It drives me crazy when the one I want to solve the most is completely illusive to me."

Karl left the office and Rhonda prepared to go to the morning briefing. Before she could get up from her chair, her cell phone rang. She checked the area code and realized it came from Southern Wisconsin. It wasn't her former partner, Phil Mason's, number. The only other person she could think of who might be calling was Rick Riley.

"Poh's here," she answered, anticipating news that Rick and Sue's grandchild had been born.

"R-Rhonda," Sue sobbed.

"Sue? What's the matter? Has something happened to Rick?"

"N-No, it's the baby. He isn't Bill's child. Our lawyer has kept the will in probate until the baby was born. He told us he didn't trust Connie and we should have a DNA test done as soon as the baby is born. We got the test results on Friday, but we didn't want to bother you on the weekend. We're contesting the will. It isn't right for Connie and her bastard to profit from Bill's death. It's not like we want the money for ourselves, but we don't want her to have it."

"I thought you all got along quite well."

"So did we, but as soon as the memorial service was over, she moved back to Illinois with her parents. At first it didn't bother us. I mean, what girl wants to go through a pregnancy without her mother? It wasn't long before she stopped responding to our emails and answering our phone calls. I resorted to writing her a long letter saying we wanted to be in the baby's life. Her response was in the form of an instant message, using words I wouldn't repeat in polite company. The gist of it was she wanted nothing more to do with us and she was changing her email address and her phone number. That was when we contacted our lawyer. I thank God Connie's mother called us when the baby was born. We went down to the hospital with a court order in hand. Luckily, Connie had to have a C-Section, so we had time to get the order. I was afraid she would disappear with the baby before we could get him tested."

"I'm so sorry, Sue. Is there anything I can do?"

"I'm sure Connie had something to do with Bill's murder. You must keep looking to find out what happened. If she didn't do it herself, she had someone do it for her."

Rhonda assured her the case had not gone cold and they were still working on any lead they could get. By the time the call ended, the morning meeting was over.

"Missed you at the meeting," Karl said, as he and Jen entered the office.

"I had a last-minute call. To say I'm shaken is an understatement."

"What are you talking about?" Jen asked.

"Sue Riley just called, Connie had the baby and I'm afraid all hell is about to break loose. Rick and Sue's lawyer has kept the will tied up until the baby was born. Long story short, the baby doesn't belong to Bill. There's

117

going to be a nasty battle over the will. We know everything was left to Connie and the baby. Depending how the court rules, it's possible she won't get anything. It's not going to be pretty. I can't say I'm sorry for Connie, I couldn't warm up to her, but I do worry about her family and that innocent baby."

"Are you thinking Connie might have had something to do with Bill's murder?"

"I'm not sure, but Rick and Sue are. What I'd like to know is who is the father of Connie's baby. It's possible our mystery man had something to do with it. I need to add this information to the file and see what comes out of it, I'd also like to get a copy of the DNA test Rick and Sue had done. Once we do, we can check it against the national DNA registry. We might get a hit that could lead to our murderer."

Karl nodded. "I think you might be onto something, Considering the will was filed one day before Billy and Connie were married is damning enough, but the ink was hardly dry on it before Billy was dead. It's just too convenient to be a coincidence. It sounds like Connie was looking for someone to support her and her child for the rest of their lives. Unfortunately, she was greedy enough not to want Billy to be part of their lives, so as soon as the marriage was legal, she did away with the one fly in the ointment. She had to know Billy would ask for a DNA test, especially if the kid didn't look like him. If we can find the man who fathered the baby, it's possible we will find the man who murdered Billy. The problem is our chief suspect is in the wind. We don't even know his real name."

Rhonda agreed with Karl. As she entered the information in the file, she contemplated the implications of the information she'd received from Sue. After typing Connie's name as the baby's mother, she thought about Sue's suspicions. She quickly added, is Connie involved in the murder, followed by four question marks.

~ * ~

Mark waited for Rhonda in the parking lot of the Sheriff's office.

Tonight, they were going to a combination birthday and going away party for Tyson. Tomorrow he would be flying out to celebrate his birthday with friends in Brazil.

He wished he could take Rhonda on an exotic vacation for their wedding anniversary but with her job it wasn't something that could be done spontaneously. It was something that required months of planning. Instead, he booked a room for them at the Excalibur for the weekend. It would be a few days late, but he knew Rhonda would understand.

As soon as Rhonda came out to his vehicle, he could tell something was weighing heavily on her mind. "What's wrong?" he asked once she attached her seat belt.

"I had a call from Sue Riley this morning. Connie's baby was born last month."

"Don't you mean Bill's baby?"

Rhonda shook her head. He could see tears in her eyes which confused him even more.

"Rick and Sue's lawyer insisted on a DNA test. There is no way Bill could be his father. This throws a monkey wrench into the whole case. All that money Bill left her and the baby is now being contested. It looks like Connie won't be getting one penny of the money she was planning on having. Rick and Sue don't need the money, since they received a sizeable inheritance from Bill. They don't want Connie to profit from Bill's death."

Mark took a moment to absorb the information Rhonda relayed to him. "I can understand how they feel. I just worry about how she will be able to support him as a single mother with no skills."

"I'm concerned about that as well. It makes it imperative we find out who fathered the child, so he can be held responsible. Unfortunately, once we find him, we'll be likely to find Bill's killer. I've already requested the DNA from the baby, along with that of Connie. Hopefully, from there we will get a profile to send to CODIS. If all the talk shows can find the father of a child, why shouldn't we be able to do the same in solving a crime?"

"I was going to keep this as a surprise, but I think I should tell you now. I know the weekend sounds a long way off, but this should give you something to look forward to. For our anniversary, I booked a weekend package at the Excalibur."

"You are so sweet. By the time this week is over, I'm going to need it."

~ * ~

The evening was a great celebration. Dinner was held at Firefly with several of Tyson's closest friends. As usual, Tyson insisted on being the host and paying for everything.

Throughout the evening, he regaled them with stories of his previous visits to Brazil and the friends he'd made there.

In a way, Rhonda envied her friend his ability to travel to exotic locations for luxurious vacations. She knew that on the salaries of a coach and a cop such things would be impossible, but it was fun to live vicariously through their friend.

"Along with my birthday," Tyson announced, "I have it on good authority that my friends, Mark and Rhonda Pohs, are celebrating their wedding anniversary this week. Please join me in a toast to the happy couple."

Everyone got to their feet and raised their glasses in salute, causing Rhonda to blush when people started to chant, "Speech, speech, speech."

Rhonda was glad when it was Mark who stood up. "I'm the luckiest guy, being married to this lovely lady. If I were to say it's been an easy road, I'd be lying. What it hasn't been is boring. We've been married for ten of the most exciting years of my life. Here's to another ten and many more after that."

Everyone again toasted them, prompting Rhonda to get to her feet as well. She didn't like speaking in public, but two glasses of sangria bolstered her confidence.

"Without Mark in my life, I would never have had the courage to pursue the job I love, even if at times things are trying. I know I'm not always the easiest person to live with, but without Mark's love, I would have quit years ago."

After the next toast, Mark took her in his arms and kissed her tenderly in front of everyone present. She knew she should have been embarrassed. Instead, she was glowing with love, not only for her husband, but for the friends who became important to them since they relocated to Las Vegas.

Chapter Seventeen

The next morning, Rhonda returned to work, still reeling from the previous evening at Firefly as well as the promise of the fantastic weekend Mark planned for her. The euphoria she felt only moments earlier evaporated as everyone was talking about the new developments in the Billy Roller case. Memories and future expectations gave way to the reality of the life she'd chosen, to say nothing about the case she desperately wanted to solve.

"I'm glad you had a good night, because this afternoon you're going to be flying out to Rockford to interrogate Connie Riley."

Karl's unexpected announcement shattered Rhonda's dreams of the weekend Mark planned. On the other hand, the excitement of getting the chance to interview Connie was exhilarating. "Are you sure?"

"Positive. Now that we know the baby doesn't belong to Billy, I think it's time for us to talk to Connie and see if she can shed any light on his murder."

Even though she knew Mark would be disappointed, Rhonda felt like a kid on Christmas morning waiting to open all the presents from Santa. She was more than ready to return to the Midwest and have a woman-to-woman talk with Connie. She prayed this wouldn't be a wild goose chase.

Once she got home, she packed a bag and called Mark to inform him about her trip to Illinois. "I'm sorry about this weekend, but Jen and I need to fly out to Rockford to interview Connie. I don't know how long this is going to take. I…"

"Ssh honey. Plans were made to be broken. It won't be hard to cancel and reschedule later. I know how important solving this case is to you. It's just as important to me. Bill was special, not only because of his music but he was generous to a fault, to say nothing of having a winning personality. Be careful and keep in touch."

An hour later, Karl pulled up with Jen already in his car. After stowing her weekender in the trunk, Rhonda slid into the back seat of the vehicle.

"Did you get in touch with Mark?" Jen asked.

"I did. I knew he made plans for our anniversary weekend. I could tell he was disappointed, but he knows me too well. He said plans were made to be broken. We can always reschedule. How about Paul, did you reach him?"

"I caught him between meetings. I can't say he was happy, since he has some clients he needs to host this weekend, but he did understand. With him being with us when Billy was found, he wants this case solved as much as we do."

It didn't take them long to make it to the airport for their flight to Rockford. Karl left them off at the sidewalk surrounding the airport and told them to let him know when they would be flying back. "In addition to the flight," he continued, "you'll be staying at the Marriott."

Rhonda longed for the days when the Clock Tower had been the place for weekend getaways and conferences. Of course, it had been closed and torn down several years earlier.

It took an hour to get through the TSA check and wait for their flight to be called. Their fellow passengers were lamenting the money they'd lost at the casinos as well as the end of their vacations. For Rhonda and Jen, it wasn't the end of a vacation, but hopefully the end of a murder investigation.

Because of the difference in time zones, the three-hour flight didn't arrive until well after six. Thankfully, the hotel provided a shuttle from the airport, eliminating the need to rent a car and navigate a strange city at night.

The double room at the hotel had two queen size beds and a pool view. Once they were settled, calls were made to Mark and Paul to let them know they'd arrived safely and where they would be staying while in Rockford.

"How long do you think this is going to take?" Jen asked, once she hung up from talking with Paul.

"We'll have to talk to the local cops tomorrow and have them go with us to where Connie is staying. Technically, we don't have any authority here.

We can only hope Connie will be receptive and will come in with us to be interviewed. If not, who knows how long this can take? At least we have great accommodations while we're here."

~ * ~

Early the next morning, Rhonda rented a car from the concierge desk at the hotel. She was pleased to see it was equipped with GPS, which would make finding, not only Connie's home, but also the local police station easier.

"We've been advised you might need help. We're ready to do anything we can to help, Detective Pohs. We're familiar with the Williams' residence because of all the people going out there after the Billy Roller murder."

Rhonda was appreciative of the offer. It didn't take long for them to meet Ken Parker and Melissa Anderson. They would be taking two cars and if Connie was receptive to coming with them, they would have room in one of the cars.

The Williams' home was sat on a quiet street in the residential area. Rhonda was a bit disappointed when it was Mrs. Williams who came to the door.

"I'm Detective Pohs from Las Vegas," Rhonda said, identifying herself. "We were wondering if we could talk to Connie."

A look of concern came over Mrs. Williams' face. "My daughter left. We were going to call the police this morning and file a missing person's report."

"What about the baby?" Jen asked.

Mrs. Williams began to cry. "She said she didn't want the baby to come with her. She left him with us. I don't know what set her off. I thought she would take him as her link to Billy."

For a moment, Rhonda was at a loss for words. "I have a feeling she left the baby behind because she knew it didn't belong to Bill."

"What do you mean it didn't belong to Billy?"

"Could we come in, so we aren't discussing this on your front step?"

Mrs. Williams nodded and led them into a cozy country kitchen. From somewhere in the house, they heard the baby crying. Mrs. Williams excused herself and went to tend to the little one. Rhonda was surprised when the woman came back not only with the baby, but also her husband.

"I thought my husband should hear what you are going to say."

Rhonda shook hands with Mr. Williams and made the rest of the formal introductions. "As I was telling your wife, the baby wasn't fathered by Bill Riley."

"What does this do to the inheritance for Connie and Benjamin?"

"I'm sorry to say the Riley's are contesting it. We've concluded Connie married Bill under false pretenses. I'm certain she knew Bill wasn't the father when she married him. It's more than a coincidence they were married, the will was registered, and Bill was killed in less than forty-eight hours. Has Connie said anything to make you think she might have been involved?"

As Rhonda could have predicted, Mrs. Williams cried while Mr. Williams' expression mirrored anger.

"Are you saying my daughter wanted her husband dead?" he questioned.

"I'm afraid so. We weren't heading in this direction until we got the report from the Riley's lawyer," Jen replied.

"By any chance, do you know this young man?" Rhonda asked, taking out the picture she'd been carrying around for months.

The color drained from Mrs. Williams' face as she looked at the picture. "That is Wade Johnston. His parents lived next door to us when the kids went to high school. Of course, just before his mother disappeared, his father bought a farm and sold the house. How is it you have a picture of him?"

"We have several pictures of him. He always seems to be in the background in a lot of shots of Connie and Bill together. Have you seen him recently?"

Mr. Williams stared at the picture in disbelief. "He's been Connie's rock through this whole nightmare. He was here just before Connie left to get her head together."

While Rhonda and Jen tried to console Mrs. Williams, the uniformed officers asked Mr. Williams for a description of the car Connie was driving, as well as the same information for Wade.

"Do you think the two of them took off together?" Mr. Williams asked.

"It's possible," Rhonda replied, leaving Jen to continue consoling Mrs. Williams. "We learned that Wade Johnston has driver's licenses in several states, each with a different name. They could be driving a different vehicle now. Considering we have descriptions of both vehicles; we can put out an all-points bulletin. Right now, they aren't wanted for anything other than questioning, but the fact they disappeared doesn't bode well for them."

The baby began to fuss, indicating he was ready to be fed. Mrs. Williams handed him to her husband, while she went to prepare a bottle.

"I tried to tell Connie she needed to be breast feeding, but she wanted no part of it," Mr. Williams said as he soothed the baby. "At the time, I couldn't understand her reasoning. Now I'm wondering if she was considering abandoning him all along."

~ * ~

By evening, the state patrol reported finding Connie's car abandoned in Love's Park, but there had been no sighting of Wade's vehicle. Knowing they had a several days head start on them, they could be anywhere.

Exhausted from the day spent with the Rockford PD, Rhonda and Jen made their way to their hotel. They had no more than ordered room service when Karl called on Rhonda's phone. Seeing who was calling, she put the call on speaker so they could both hear what Karl had to say.

"How are things going out there?"

"We've found out our guy is Wade Johnston. He went to high school with Connie. Unfortunately, they have both disappeared. The state patrol found Connie's car abandoned in one of the suburbs of Rockford. I'm hoping they don't decide to abandon Wade's vehicle. We have all the information on that car. Sooner or later, they're going to be found. With luck they won't put up much of a fight about being brought in."

"What about the baby?"

"She's abandoned him as well. She left him with her parents before she disappeared. I have a feeling she never wanted the baby and planned to leave him as soon as possible. I also think she believes no one knows about Wade. It's entirely possible he's the baby's father."

"It's possible you're right. I must admit I didn't have high hopes when you left for Rockford, but I think it was a good move. What about her parents, do you think they're in on it?"

"It's highly doubtful. When we got there, they were getting ready to file a missing person's report. Connie left their home on Saturday, and they haven't heard from her since. They were afraid something happened to her. I think the knowledge the baby didn't belong to Bill came as a total shock to them. The one I feel sorry for is that little baby. He didn't ask to be born. Now it's possible he'll grow up without either of his parents."

"Do you think Connie and Wade were in on this together?"

"It's beginning to look that way. Unfortunately, we won't know for sure until we locate them."

"Stay as long as you need to. When you find them, I'll have an extradition order drawn up for them. I'm sure, just like Axton, they will be fighting returning to Nevada."

Rhonda agreed completely. When she finished the call, she lay back on the bed. The last thing she wanted to do was to eat, but they already ordered room service. Once it was delivered, she was certain it would be more appealing. Right now, she wanted nothing more than to take a nap.

Chapter Eighteen

The ringing of the hotel room phone woke Rhonda at five AM. She knew if anything was wrong at home, she would have been contacted on her cell.

Trying not to sound as though she'd just awakened, she answered with her usual 'Pohs Here'.

In the other bed, Jen sat up, looking like she was disoriented from the early morning wake up call. "Detective Pohs, this is James Sorenson. I'm the commander of the night shift for the Rockford PD. We just received a call from Oklahoma. Wade Johnston and Connie Riley were involved in an accident last night. It's a good thing we put out the description of their vehicle nationwide. We're making arrangements for you to fly out of O'Hare at nine this morning. Our officers will be at your hotel in about an hour to take you, so you don't have to worry about leaving your vehicle at the airport."

"We'll be ready and waiting in the lobby. What time will they be here?"

"We're planning on six. I hope that gives you enough time."

"It should work."

"What should work?" Jen asked.

"Wade and Connie were picked up after an accident in Oklahoma last night. Someone from the Rockford PD will be picking us up in the lobby at six."

"That doesn't give us much time. What about breakfast?"

"We'll have to pick something up at the airport. More important than eating is coffee. I need a cup right now. Thank goodness they have a coffee maker in the room. Why don't you go in and take a shower, while I pack and make the coffee?"

By six they were packed and waiting in the lobby. Fortified by the coffee, they were ready to be picked up and taken to the airport.

"We could have taken the bus," Rhonda said when the two officers from the day before picked them up.

"We're going with you. It will be less expensive than the four of us taking the bus," Ken said. "Melissa and I are both acquainted with Wade and will be able to make a positive identification."

"Besides, you can't get this on the bus." Melissa produced a McDonalds bag along with a carrier of cups of coffee. "I didn't know what you'd like, so I grabbed a couple of everything on the breakfast menu. Since they don't serve food on planes anymore, I think you would need it."

"What about you?" Jen asked.

"I drove over from the restaurant giving Ken a chance to eat. I'll be eating with the two of you."

Rhonda could feel her mouth water at the thought of something more substantial than the hotel coffee she made while they were getting ready.

Once they were out on the highway and finished their breakfast, Rhonda posed the question that was burning on her mind. "How well do you know Wade?"

Ken laughed at her comment. "I doubt there's an officer in town who doesn't know him. He was a hell of a wild kid. I've picked him up for underage drinking, drag racing, marijuana, and for being a Peeping Tom. How about you, Melissa, what have you collared him for?"

"Just about the same list. He was a minor at the time and his old man bailed him out. Mr. Johnston was a very wealthy man. It's too bad he didn't live long enough to enjoy his retirement."

"Was?" Jen questioned. "How did he die? Was he sick?"

"Hardly. It was a nasty accident. Right after his wife disappeared, he had one of those spa tubs installed. Apparently, he slipped while getting in and hit his head. He drowned. His body wasn't found until about two days later when Wade came home and discovered him. At the time we wondered if it was an accident, but Wade said he'd been out of town when it happened."

"Sounds quite convenient to me. What happened to his estate? For that matter, why didn't anyone want to investigate it further?"

"Like I said earlier, his wife disappeared about five years ago. A year later, old man Johnston filed for divorce, leaving Wade the only heir to everything. He was always a spoiled brat. As I recall, he lorded it over everyone about how rich he was going to be someday. In my opinion, wherever the wife is, she's better off without him."

The wheels in Rhonda's mind began to turn. She wondered how a woman could leave her teenage son with a man she could no longer stand. Was the woman living somewhere other than Illinois or had she died? If so, it was possible hers was an unsolved mystery. Added to that were the circumstances of her husband's death. What if they'd both been murdered?

"I might be out of line here, but what's the possibility Mrs. Johnston didn't just disappear, but was murdered? The same holds true for her husband."

"I've always wondered about the same possibility," Ken said. "I never quite bought his story about her disappearance, but we had no reason to believe she was murdered. It's hard to prove a murder without a body. As for her husband, the same holds true. As for his death, the coroner ruled it accidental, end of story. Wade was shaken over finding his father's body, plus he had an airtight alibi. In other words, cases closed. I pray Mrs. Johnston is living somewhere far away from that jerk she was married to."

Their conversation made the miles between Rockford and Chicago melt away. Before they knew it, they were parked in the long-term lot and taking the shuttle bus to the terminal.

~ * ~

Once their plane landed, they were met by two officers from the Oklahoma Highway Patrol.

"We were told there were four of you coming, so we brought a van. We just got word the prisoners have been taken to the Brady County Jail in

Chickasaw. We have reservations for you at the Hampton Inn. Do you want to go there or the jail first?"

"The jail," Rhonda said. "We can always check in at the hotel later. How did you apprehend them?"

"From what we were told, they were traveling on the H.E. Bailey Turnpike and ran the toll booth going about ninety. One of our officers took up the chase and they tried to outrun him. That was when they blew a tire and ended up flipping the car and landing upside down in the median. It happened about eight o'clock last night, but we had to use the jaws of life to extricate them from the vehicle. From there they were taken to the hospital to be treated for their injuries before they were transferred to jail. They just got to jail about an hour ago. By the time we'd run their plates, we found out they were wanted on murder charges. Do you mind if I ask who they're suspected of murdering? I mean, they're just a couple of kids, probably out for a joy ride in Daddy's fancy car, aren't they?"

Rhonda hesitated for a moment. This case haunted her for over six months and now, within a matter of minutes, she would be confronting the two people who had become her chief suspects.

"Are you familiar with the Billy Roller case?"

"Are you kidding? Who hasn't heard about it? It's no wonder I thought I recognized your names. I saw enough coverage on that case, including that fiasco in Idaho. I'm glad you got the son of a bitch who laced the candy with cocaine. I was hoping he was the bastard who killed Billy. My kids were devastated about his death. I even liked his music. I didn't put two and two together but wasn't his wife's name Connie?"

"It was. She's Connie Riley now because that's Bill's real name."

"Damn, it's no wonder I didn't recognize her. I guess I expected her last name to be Roller."

"You mentioned an accident," Jen said. "How badly were they injured?"

"Connie Riley has a broken arm and a broken collarbone. She was treated and released since she didn't need hospitalization. It's the same with her companion. He has some facial cuts as well as a broken ankle."

"I didn't want them injured," Rhonda admitted. "At least neither of them are in any shape to try to take our lives."

~ * ~

Once they arrived at the County Jail, Rhonda opted to question Connie first. Nervous anticipation filled her senses as she waited for the matron to bring Connie into the interrogation room.

"What are you doing here, bitch?" Connie asked as soon as she recognized Rhonda.

"You know why I'm here. Did you think you would get away with killing your husband?"

"I didn't kill Billy and you know it. I have an airtight alibi."

"Of course you do. You didn't wield the knife, but I'm sure you and your boyfriend were in this together. I'm certain you didn't think the Riley's would demand a DNA test once the baby was born, but they did. Your baby wasn't fathered by Bill Riley. I'll bet once we run Wade Johnston's DNA, we'll find out he's the proud papa."

"I don't believe you."

"Didn't you know the Rileys had a court order for the baby's DNA?"

"I-I don't remember. I thought they would be chomping at the bit to see the kid, but they didn't even come down. I figured they'd take the brat back to Wisconsin."

"Well, they didn't. Instead, they found out he's not their grandson. As for that big pay out you were expecting from Bill's will, it won't be coming either. They've contested the will and there will be no money for you. Knowing that, do you want to make a statement?"

"No, bitch. I want a fuckin' lawyer."

"Take me back to my cell." She said to the matron, who was monitoring their conversation. "I don't want to talk to this bitch any longer."

Rhonda watched as Connie was taken away. She'd expected the girl to deny everything. Instead, she lawyered up. It was evident she thought a good lawyer would get her out of the inevitable charge of murder.

~ * ~

It took only a matter of minutes before Wade was brought into the interrogation room. She was pleased to have Ken join her. He could identify Wade from personal association, while she would know him anywhere from the pictures she'd been staring at for the past six months. The man who was wheeled into the room looked exactly like the pictures, except for the stitched-up cuts on his face and two black eyes.

"Who the hell are you?" he asked as soon as he saw Rhonda.

"I'm Detective Rhonda Pohs and I'm sure you know your friend, Ken."

"I didn't do shit in Illinois. Why in the hell are you here, Kenny boy?"

"You'd better watch your mouth, Wade. You're in a boatload of trouble. Let's see, in Oklahoma, you're under arrest for speeding and reckless driving, to say nothing of trying to elude an officer of the law. In Nevada, you're wanted for the murder of Bill Riley. As far as Illinois is concerned, I have a feeling you know more about the death of your father and the disappearance of your mother than you're letting on."

"You don't know nothin'. My old lady left the old man, and he slipped getting into the bathtub."

"I honestly don't care about any of this," Rhonda said. "What I want to know is why you killed Bill Riley?"

"I bet you would. That damn fucker was so full of himself. He got exactly what he deserved. He was such a goody two-shoes. I was the one who told Connie to cozy up to him. The dumb bitch went and got herself pregnant. I told her to stay on the damn pill, but she didn't want anything to do with it. She said it made her get fat. It sure made things rough on me. I like to do it bareback. Of course, little Billy always wore a condom. She did a lot of fast talking to get him to believe his condom broke. That bastard couldn't marry her fast enough. After that, it was a piece of cake to kill him."

"Are you saying you killed Billy?"

"Sure itch, why not? I might fry but I ain't gonna fry alone. It was all Connie's idea. She wanted all that money Billy had. She convinced him the brat was his and when he said he'd marry her, she convinced him to write a will leaving everything to her. It was the perfect plan, but the dumb bitch decided she didn't want anything to do with Billy's folks. If she'd played it nice, they would have never insisted on that DNA test. We had it all planned, once she got the money, she'd take the kid up to visit Billy's folks then forget to come back."

Rhonda held up her hand to silence Wade. "How did you know about the DNA test? When I mentioned it to Connie, she was shocked."

"She's a damn good actress. Right after the kid was born, she got a certified letter with the results of the test. Hell, she didn't need a DNA test to know that. She knew, as well as I did that the kid belonged to me."

"I'm sorry I interrupted you. What else can you tell me about Bill's murder?"

"Let's see, where was I. Oh yes, I know. The best idea I ever had was talking that no mind Axton into lacing the candy with cocaine. By the time I got into that dressing room, Billy was high as a kite."

Rhonda took a moment to absorb everything Wade told her. She'd never had anyone confess to murder with such a calm demeanor before. "You do know your right to remain silent, don't you?"

"Of course I do, bitch, those fools were reading me my rights when they pulled me out of the wreck. Damn, I liked that car, too. It was my old man's, and he always bought the best."

"As long as you feel like talking, how about telling us what happened to your mother?" Ken asked.

"That bitch had it made with my old man. He had tons of money, and she never wanted for anything. So what if she had to put up with his affairs and getting knocked around a little bit. Then one night she pushed him too far. The next morning the old man had me help him bury her in the back yard, where he was building a gazebo. It was something she harped on wanting to have for several years. At least she got what she wanted, just not the way she wanted it. If you can talk those suckers who bought the house from me into digging up the gazebo they fell in love with, you'll find her. I didn't kill her That was the old man's doing."

"Maybe you didn't kill her, but you did help hide the body. That's a crime in Illinois. Now, why don't you tell me about your father?"

"What about him? The bastard slipped and fell in that fancy bathtub the old lady wanted. Guess she got her revenge. By the time I got home and found him, he stunk to high heaven. He was all bloated. I mean he was a fat pig to begin with and to see him like that made me sick to my stomach. I've been up front with you about what I've done, but I'll be damned if I confess to something I didn't do. Karma is a bitch, or so they tell me."

Ken was grinning like the cat who swallowed the canary. He'd closed a cold case but couldn't charge Wade with his parents' murders.

"Wade Johnston, you're under arrest for the murder of Bill Riley, AKA Billy Roller. You're going to be extradited to Nevada to stand trial."

Rhonda didn't think she'd ever get to say those words. She couldn't believe how relieved she felt. She'd dreamed of this moment, but it was so much better than anything she ever anticipated.

"I want a deal," Wade said. "I'll go back to Nevada but when I get there, I want a fuckin' lawyer and a fuckin' deal. I know more than anyone knows and I'm ready to spill my guts."

Rhonda exchanged a bewildered glance with Ken before looking toward the one-way mirror where he knew Jen was watching the interview.

"I think we're done here. We'll be arranging to have you extradited to Nevada and take things from there. You might want to hire a lawyer out there. If you can't afford one, one will be appointed for you."

"You bet I'll be hiring my own lawyer, bitch. I know how those court-appointed pricks are. They can't get a job with the big law firms, so they defend the poor jerks who can't afford a lawyer. Once I tell him everything, I'll get a deal and be out of jail with a slap on the wrist."

"If that happens," Ken said, "I'll be waiting to arrest you as an accessory to the murder of your mother. If I could, I'd add the murder of your father to your charges."

Rhonda could see Wade trying to control his anger. With his broken ankle, he couldn't get up from his wheelchair, but clenched his fists over and over again.

"Try it, you son of a bitch, and I'll make you look like a fool. I admit I helped the old man bury the body of my mother but as much as I wanted him dead, I didn't do him in. He was a bastard, but he was paying my bills. No one kills the golden goose. I certainly didn't think he'd leave everything to me. He always told me he was leaving everything to charity. I suppose he did that so I wouldn't try to kill him for his money."

The interview was over. Rhonda asked to speak to Connie again. As she expected, the girl was as belligerent as she'd been earlier.

"I told you I don't want to talk to you, bitch."

"You don't have to say anything. Connie Riley, you are under arrest for the murder of your husband, Bill Riley. You have the right to remain silent, anything…"

"I know all that Miranda bullshit."

"Since you do, you also know you can get your own lawyer. We're arranging for you to return to Nevada to stand trial."

Tears formed in Connie's eyes. It was the first emotion she'd seen from the girl, as even at the memorial service she stood dry-eyed. It was evident her tears were for herself and no one else.

"I didn't kill Billy. It was that bastard Wade."

"We know what happened. Wade told us everything."

Connie's eyes went wide in shock. "That bastard."

With that one statement, she refused to say anything more.

~ * ~

"You look beat," Jen said when Rhonda finally exited the interrogation room.

"That took a lot out of me. I don't know if Wade was spouting off a lot of BS, but it will be interesting to hear what he has to say once we get him back to Nevada. One thing is certain, he'll be able to hire the best lawyer available. From what Ken tells me, his father left him independently wealthy.

I'm sure he promised Connie the same thing when she found out she was pregnant."

Ken suggested they get some dinner, but Rhonda insisted on calling Karl before they did anything.

"Where are you?" Karl asked as soon as he answered Rhonda's call.

"Chickasha, Oklahoma. We just arrested Connie Riley and Wade Johnston. Can you arrange for them to be extradited back to Nevada? They were involved in an accident last night after a high-speed chase on the H.E. Bailey Turnpike. I doubt if either of them should be on a commercial flight."

"I'll send a prison van to pick them up along with both a male and female officer. How are you and Jen holding up?"

"We both feel like we've been on one of those crazy rides at the top of the Stratosphere Hotel. We got the call at five this morning and by six we were on our way to O'Hare. After that it seems like all hell broke loose. We were met in Oklahoma City by two of the county officers and brought here. Connie wasn't talking, but Wade couldn't shut up. We have it all on tape and I'll be bringing copies of it when we fly out. I'm just ready to go home but not until I'm sure Wade and Connie are on their way back to Nevada."

"I think you should be prepared for the press. You know how they can be. This is a big story and if any of them get so much as a whiff of it, they'll be all over you like stink on shit."

Hearing Karl use such language came as a surprise, but after the interviews with Wade and Connie, she was getting used to it.

"I'm expecting them. Right now, I feel like I could go back to the hotel and sleep for the next week. If you need us, we'll be at the Hampton Inn in Chickasha, Of course, you also have our cell numbers."

Karl repeated his warning before ending the call.

"Are you ready to go?" Jen asked. "Ken and Melissa are working on getting the four of us a vehicle so we can get something to eat."

"I'm as ready as I'll ever be. Karl is concerned about the press. I'm afraid the locals have gotten wind of this and will be waiting for us. I've been anticipating it, but I honestly don't expect much. There might be some locals, but I doubt there will be anyone from the national networks. Let's face it, they were just apprehended last night."

Jen shook her head in disagreement, making Rhonda wonder if her partner was right. Nevertheless, she prepared to go out and face the locals.

As soon as they walked out of the County Jail Building, there were sound trucks, reporters and cameramen from the major network waiting for them.

"Detective Pohs, is it true you and Detective Sims have made an arrest in the Billy Roller murder case?"

"Yes, we have, but we're not at liberty to give you any details until the suspects have been extradited to Nevada and arraigned."

"You said 'suspects'. Are we to assume there are more than one?"

"As I said before, we're not at liberty to give you any details. The suspects will be returned to Nevada. There they will be formally charged and arraigned. Thank you for your continued coverage of this investigation. Now, if you will excuse me, my partner and I have had a very long day, and we need to get something to eat and some well-deserved rest."

The sea of reporters seemed to part like the Red Sea for Moses, allowing Rhonda, Jen, Ken and Melissa to go to their waiting vehicle.

~ * ~

They'd just put in their order for dinner when Rhonda's phone rang. Before answering she checked the caller ID and realized it came from Mark.

"Hi Honey," she greeted.

"Do I have the right number?" Mark teased. "My wife always answers her phone with Pohs here."

"Yes, you have the right number. I knew it was you and right now I'm tired of being Detective Pohs."

"Are you okay? I just saw the special bulletin on TV. You look like hell."

"I love you, too. As for you seeing the bulletin, what were you doing watching TV in the middle of the day?"

"I usually have the news channel on when I don't have a class. When the special bulletin came across the screen, I paid closer attention. I'm very worried about you. Did you apprehend the suspects? Were you in danger?"

"No, I didn't apprehend them. As of last night, I was still in Rockford at the hotel. At that time, we had no idea where to find them. We got a call this morning at five AM saying they'd been in a high-speed chase in Oklahoma that ended in an accident. We flew down this morning and I arrested them for Bill's murder. Now we're waiting for Karl to finish the paperwork and send someone to pick them up and escort them back to Nevada."

"I knew you were evasive when you were talking to the press, but can you tell me who you arrested?"

"Not right now. I can tell you more when I get home. I need to keep the identities of the suspects quiet until they are arraigned. You understand this is a high-profile case and the less you know the better. You've had enough press coverage over this case. Once they realize you don't know anything, they should leave you alone."

"Of course, you're right. I'm just anxious to have this over and done with. I'm also lonely, I want you back home."

"I want the same thing. As soon as Karl sends out the team to bring them back to Nevada, I'll be on a plane back to Vegas and my own bed."

"I'll have it ready and waiting for you. I love you."

"I love you, too."

Dreamy eyed over the conversation with Mark, she ended the call.

"I don't have to ask who you were talking to, do I?" Jen teased when Rhonda ended the call.

"I doubt it. Mark was watching the news in his office when they put the special bulletin on the screen. He was worried."

"I suppose I should call Paul before he sees it."

Ken laughed at their conversation. "Are you gals married?" he finally managed to ask.

"I'm married, but Jen has a special boyfriend," Rhonda explained. "The guys tend to be a bit overprotective of us. I guess, in the past, I've given Mark enough cause for worry. On one of the cases I was involved in back in

Wisconsin, I got shot. It wasn't serious, but Mark was a basket case over it."

"Now I know how I recognized your name," Melissa declared. "I heard about the cases in Wisconsin. I didn't put two and two together until now. You've had quite a successful career."

Jen smiled. "There's a reason we make such a good team. I'm learning the ropes of being a homicide detective and I couldn't have a better teacher than Rhonda. She's the best and it's so easy to work with and learn from her."

Chapter Nineteen

Rhonda and Jen took the opportunity to sleep in. They were lingering over their morning coffee when they received a call from Ken and Melissa telling them they were preparing to leave for the airport.

They left the coffee shop to meet Ken and Melissa and say goodbye. Rhonda ached to be going home as well. She knew she had a job to finish. She couldn't leave until Connie and Wade were in the custody of the Clark County Sheriff's Deputies. As soon as the transfer was made, they would be free to catch the next flight home.

By the time they met Ken and Melissa in the lobby, it was almost time for them to catch the shuttle for the airport.

"Thank you for all your help with this case." Rhonda said as the shuttle bus pulled up.

"I'm the one who should be thanking you," Ken said as he shook Rhonda's hand as well as Jens. "We solved a cold case as to what happened to Donna Johnston. Our next step is to dig up that patio and give credence to Wade's story. We'll keep you posted on how we come out. Of course, we'll be watching what happens in Nevada."

"Ken and I will contact the Williams family," Melissa added. "I know it won't be easy for them, but I doubt they will be giving up little Benjamin. At least they'll know what happened to their daughter."

Rhonda and Jen shook hands with Melissa and wished her luck. They'd no more than pulled away when Rhonda's' phone rang.

"Pohs here," she answered.

"Rhonda, it's Karl. I wanted to let you know the officers with the van from here have been delayed. They ran into a bad accident just outside of

Santa Fe. It's going to take a while for the state patrol to clear the Interstate, so they had to pull off. It was late last night so they stayed at a hotel and got a fresh start this morning. They won't be getting in until late tonight. Can you book them rooms at the hotel where you're staying? It will delay picking up the prisoners until tomorrow morning, but it's best if they are rested for the trip back."

"I don't know what to say. I can understand the delay. I also don't think it's wise to pick up the prisoners tonight. The officers from Rockford just checked out, so I'll book their rooms under our names. I'm thinking, maybe Jen and I should drive back with them. I mean four drivers are better than two."

"That's all taken care of. Considering how belligerent the prisoners sounded on the tapes you sent, we thought it best to have four officers to transfer them. That way two will be guarding them all the time. I'm anxious to get Johnston back here and confer with his lawyer. It will be interesting to know what else he has to tell us regarding the Billy Roller murder. As soon as the prisoners are in the van, I want you and Jen to catch the first flight back. We need to compare notes before we talk to the lawyers for these two prisoners."

After a couple of minutes of small talk, Rhonda ended the call. From the smile on Jen's face, she could tell the delay wasn't a big disappointment.

"I like this little town and would enjoy doing some exploring. I picked up a brochure while you were in the shower. Did you see the movie A Christmas Story?"

Inwardly, Rhonda groaned. Usually, she and Mark had similar tastes in movies, but one movie she couldn't stand was A Christmas Story. While Mark watched the marathon every Christmas Eve, Rhonda took the time to wrap presents or relax with a good book.

"I've seen it. I watched it once with Mark. I had nightmares about the kid with the gun and the pink bunny pajamas for weeks. I haven't watched it since."

"Well, too bad. They have a monument to that movie, and I want to see it. If Mark is as much of a fan as you say, it will be fun to send him a picture of you in front of it."

An image of herself standing in front of the kid in the bunny suit crossed her mind as she started to smile. "You're right, Mark would get a hoot out of it. While I'm extending our stay and rebooking the other two rooms, why don't you rent us a car? I'll also let the locals know about the delay."

~ * ~

After they stopped for breakfast, they drove around the quaint town. She thought how different the area was from the fields around town with dark rich dirt to the red clay of Oklahoma. There was no comparison to the glitz and glamor of the Las Vegas Strip.

With Jen doing the driving, Rhonda was able to relax. She thought she only closed her eyes for a second when she heard Jen say, "Wake up, sleepy head. We're here."

Rhonda opened her eyes to see a gigantic replica of the leg lamp from A Christmas Story complete with the packing box. "This certainly wasn't what I was expecting. You're right, we need to get pictures of us in front of it. It's too bad we don't have fishnet stockings so we can pretend to be just like the lamp."

"You do have a weird sense of humor. I'm glad I didn't tell you what the statue was. The look on your face was amazing."

They spent the next forty-five minutes taking and sending pictures. Rhonda added a note about the delay promising to call Mark later in the evening.

~ * ~

The rest of the day seemed to fly by. They were just preparing to leave for dinner when Rhonda had a call from the officers who would be escorting Connie and Wade back to Nevada, to meet them at the sheriff's office.

They were lucky enough to trade the sedan they'd rented earlier in the day for a van that would hold all six of them. Once everyone was settled in the van, they went out to get their dinner. Once they ordered, the officers from Clark County had several questions about the prisoners they would be picking up the next day.

Rhonda was pleased to see the office was smart enough to send two men and two women. Not only did it make the hotel accommodations easier, but with two women to watch Connie, she could be escorted by both officers for comfort stops along the way.

"I've studied this case since day one," Officer Marcia Karsten said. "I saw all the tabloid pictures of Billy's wife. She looked like a frail little thing. I can't believe she was the mastermind behind his murder."

Rhonda agreed with Marcia's statement, and it corresponded with her first opinion of Connie Williams-Riley. "I know what you mean. Unfortunately, the girl I met yesterday was not the sweet young thing she wanted to portray. Her parents are delightful people, but she's a conniving little bitch with a mouth to match."

"What can you tell me about the other prisoner?" Officer John Meyers asked.

"I can't get a read on him," Jen replied. "I watched while Rhonda was interrogating him, and he couldn't shut up. He wanted to take credit for the murder then insisted it was all Connie's idea. He also thinks he has some information that will get him off with a light sentence. I have a feeling he's delusional. None of it makes any sense. It's like he wants it all to be about himself yet still put the guilt on someone else at the same time. He's on the hook for first degree murder. No matter what he tells us, it won't make any difference when it comes time for his sentencing."

While they were discussing the prisoners they were picking up the next day, Rhonda was assessing the officers sent out from Nevada. Marcia was a petite blonde, while Sharon loomed more like an Amazon. She was a large-boned and muscular red head who looked like she could handle herself in any situation.

The men were a different story. John and his partner Alex Brown were both well-built and made Wade look like a ninety-eight-pound weakling. She was certain they would have no problem transferring the prisoners from Oklahoma to Nevada.

~ * ~

The next morning, Rhonda and Jen accompanied the officers from Clark County to pick up Connie and Wade. They arrived just after the shift change at seven-thirty.

Connie was brought out first. Seeing her, Rhonda couldn't believe this was the belligerent woman she'd seen two days earlier. It was evident jail hadn't set well with her and Rhonda wondered how she would handle a life sentence, while her son grew up without her.

"I should have known you'd be here, bitch."

Rhonda turned at the sound of Wade's voice from behind her. He was still in the wheelchair because of the cast on his ankle.

"That's right, I'm talking to you, bitch," he said when she turned to look at him. "I can't believe you got me up at this ungodly hour. I hardly had time to eat the slop they feed us here. Can't say I'm going to miss this hellhole. Maybe once we get back to Vegas, I'll get some decent chow. You gonna bring me steak and lobster, bitch?"

With the question, he put his shackled hands to his lips and blew Rhonda a kiss. The action creeped her out completely. She enjoyed watching as Alex and John attached their belly chains around his waist, attached to handcuffs. Had it not been for the cast on his ankle they would have also attached leg chains.

"See bitch, I'm a real dangerous man. They don't want me reaching out to squeeze the life out of your pretty body."

With that statement, he acted as though he wanted to lunge out of the chair toward Rhonda and Jen. All that stopped Wade was Alex pressing him back against the wheelchair.

Rather than give Wade the satisfaction of her attention, Rhonda turned back to Connie. With her arm immobilized in the cast, the belly chain was only attached to one arm. She did have leg chains attached to her ankles. Unlike Wade, she was docile rather than belligerent. She made no comment as Marcia and Sharon changed out the shackles the Brady County officer used with one they brought from Clark County.

Rhonda and Jen followed them to the van and watched as both prisoners were secured in the third row of seats behind the metal mesh partition separating them from the officers in the front two seats.

As they pulled away, Rhonda said a silent prayer of thanks that she wouldn't be making the twenty-plus hour trip back to Las Vegas listening to Wade's foul mouth.

Chapter Twenty

One of the officers from Brady County took Rhonda and Jen to the airport in Oklahoma City. Rhonda was glad they didn't need to rely on the shuttle from the hotel. The officer let them off at their terminal and they headed through the airport for the check-in procedures. She always hated the explanation she needed to give whenever she traveled for either business or pleasure.

Once they were finally cleared to board the plane, she finally relaxed. Together they made their way to the boarding area. With an hour to kill, they made their way to one of the restaurants across from where the other passengers waited for their flights to be called.

"I know it's too early for lunch and too late for breakfast. That said, the donut and coffee we had at the hotel wore off a couple of hours ago. I'm certain they won't feed us anything other than a bag of peanuts on the plane. I'm hoping we can get something here to hold us over until we get home."

Rhonda smiled at Jen. "You must have read my mind. While we check around, why don't you give Paul a call so he can meet our flight?"

"He sent me a text that Karl got ahold of him and gave him our flight information. He said he'd be waiting for us. How about Mark?"

"He's taking time off work to meet the flight. Karl contacted him as well. You know what they say, absence makes the heart grow fonder."

"I hope so, Paul wasn't thrilled about me being away so long for this case. I've talked to him every night and he keeps asking when I think I'll be home. Honestly, Rhonda, I think he's the one. He's been so supportive through this whole case, but my being out of town has put a strain on our relationship. I hope it survives."

"He seems like the perfect match for you. It's hard to be with a cop. Just ask Mark. We were married while I was still in school, so by the time I took my first job, he was stuck with me. He worries about all the stuff that goes on during an investigation, but I worry about him as well. It may not be easy to be married to a cop, but he has his own challenges working with teenagers. I'll take a bad guy over kids any day."

~ * ~

Mark pulled into the parking lot at the airport. On the seat next to him was the bouquet of flowers he'd purchased from Rhonda's favorite floral shop.

Over the past few years Rhonda traveled for her job, but she'd never been gone this long. She'd also never taken this much time to solve a crime. This case was different. Bill Riley was someone they'd known and watched grow from a pesky kid to a super star. She'd taken his murder personally and with good reason.

After finding a place to park, he hurried into the baggage claim area of the terminal. If his timing was right, her plane should be landing at the same time he entered the terminal.

He smiled to see Paul, Jen's boyfriend, waiting at the carousel where the luggage from their flight would be coming in. Like Mark, he carried a bouquet of flowers.

"I wondered if you'd be here to pick up Jen," Mark greeted Paul.

"It's been the longest few days I've ever lived through. Thank goodness I've been able to work from home the last couple of weeks so I could get time off to be here this morning. I haven't been with Jen through any other cases. Is it usually like this?"

"No two cases are alike. If you're in this for the long run, you should be prepared to go through times like this. I keep telling myself Rhonda is doing exactly what she's good at and enjoys. As far as I can see, it's the same with Jen. She's as dedicated as Rhonda when it comes to police work."

Paul's wide grin said volumes. It was possible the young man had more than flowers to give to Jen.

~ * ~

Rhonda was surprised she'd been able to sleep through most of their flight. The announcement from the captain that they would be landing soon, woke Rhonda. With the other passengers they stowed their tray tables and fastened their seatbelts for the descent into the Las Vegas Airport.

All around them their fellow travelers told her they were all tourists expecting all the things Las Vegas had to offer. She wondered if they would be as excited on their return flight when they realized they'd made large donations to the casinos rather than the big returns they expected.

The plane landed with no problems and soon Rhonda and Jen found themselves following the herd of passengers anxious to reclaim their luggage.

As soon as they entered the baggage claim area, they spotted Mark and Paul. Rhonda smiled to see they each carried a large bouquet of flowers. Suddenly, the hubbub of their fellow passengers didn't matter. The men in their lives were waiting for them and it was evident they had been missed.

To Rhonda's surprise, they'd no more than joined the guys than Paul dropped to one knee.

"I've missed you so much. I want to make sure you always come back to me. Will you marry me, Jenny?"

"Oh Paul, yes, yes, yes. I will be honored to be your wife."

With her acceptance, the people around them forgot about claiming their luggage and broke into applause and well wishes for the newly engaged couple.

Mark took Rhonda in his arms and held her as though he was afraid she might disappear. "I don't have a diamond ring for you, but I'm just as glad to have you home as Paul is to have Jen back safe and sound."

"I wasn't in any danger this time. It's great to be back home again. I know this case isn't over by a long shot, but at least we know that Connie and Wade are in custody. I'm so glad Karl sent four officers to bring them back,

I can't imagine having to put up with Wade's foul mouth for the twenty-hour drive from Oklahoma to Vegas."

"Wade? That name isn't familiar, but isn't Connie Bill's wife?"

"I'm sorry, I couldn't tell you this before. I know we don't have the complete story yet, but Wade Johnston is the mystery man in the pictures. I'm sure once we take a DNA sample from him, we'll find out he's the father of her son. It seems she was the mastermind of the murder, and he was the hitman. He says he has more to tell us, so I'm anxious to see if he was just blowing off steam. Somehow, he thinks he's going to get off with a slap on the wrist. I don't see that happening."

"Okay that's enough shop talk. What do you say we take the happy couple out for lunch? I know how you eat when you're on a case."

Chapter Twenty-one

Rhonda sat across the table from a far different Wade Johnston than the one she first met in Oklahoma. Even dressed in jail attire, he was cleanshaven, his hair had been trimmed, and his belligerent attitude seemed to be gone.

Sitting on his side of the table was a well-known lawyer. She recognized him from the various high profiled cases he'd defended in the past.

On her side of the table, Jen sat on her right and the district attorney on her left. They were all anxious to find out what information, if any, Wade thought would affect his standing with the court.

"Mr. Johnston wants to know what kind of deal you're willing to offer considering what he knows about the others associated with the murder of Billy Roller."

"Bill Riley," Rhonda corrected the lawyer.

"Whatever," the lawyer responded with a wave of his hand.

"It depends on the information he has to give us."

The lawyer and Wade engaged in a whispered conference.

"Since Mr. Johnston has already confessed to the murder or Billy Roller, or Bill Riley, whichever you prefer, we're asking for you to take the death penalty off the table."

"Depending on what Mr. Johnston has to tell us, it's a possibility."

"Look," Wade began, "I don't have anything to lose. I know I'm going down for the murder, but I don't plan to go down alone. There were three of us in it. Carlton Axton and I knew Connie from the neighborhood in Rockford. We all went to a Billy Roller concert in Chicago together. That's when Connie said she was sick and tired of her life. She told me she wanted to screw Billy, and I do mean literally screw him. Her plan was to get pregnant by him and have him marry her. We told her he wouldn't give her the time of day, but we all decided to drive out to Los Angeles to meet him. At the time we thought she was crazy. Before she met him, she had a complete makeover with my money. Once I saw her new look, I thought she might have a chance of pulling this off. The more we thought about it the more excited we became and said what the hell, let's give it a shot."

Wade paused to take a drink of the water sitting on the table.

"We thought it was going to be a great adventure and then Carlton managed to get hired as one of the roadies. After that is was easy for Connie to get close enough to Billy to get into his bed. All she could do was complain to me about how Billy always insisted on using a condom. She told me it was time we started sleeping together so she could get pregnant. She told me about the baby about a week before she told Billy. That was about the same time Billy caught Carlton doing drugs and fired his ass. Carlton was pissed to the max and told Connie she had to do something. That was when she ramped up her plan not only to tell Billy she was pregnant, get him to marry her, but also to get him to change his will, leaving everything to her.

"After Billy fired Carlton, it wasn't hard for us to think up a plan on how to discredit Billy in the eyes of his fans. Carlton knew how to get cocaine and was able to inject it into those chocolate covered cherries Billy loved so much. That would have been enough for me, but Connie said we had to get rid of him. She couldn't stand to have him touch her when she was carrying my baby, and she wanted him to be dead. It wasn't hard for me to get into his dressing room. By the time I got there he was high on cocaine and pretty much out of it. Since he wasn't used to taking any kind of drugs, it didn't take much to get him high. I slit his throat and stabbed him in the back."

Ronda was beginning to see Connie in a whole new light. "I have one question for you, Wade. If you were so close to Axton and Connie, how come none of the other band members recognized you?"

Wade laughed at her question. Once he regained his composure, he leaned forward until he was close to Rhonda. "That was easy. Connie and

Carlton were the ones who were close to Billy. I was just a fan who showed up at concerts and managed to photo bomb him and Connie. I was Carlton's dealer. I got the drugs for him and made a good profit. Besides, I don't need the money. When the old man died, he left everything to me, I was and still am independently wealthy. I certainly didn't need a job from a little prick like Billy Roller. If Billy's parents hadn't insisted on that damn DNA test, we would have been on easy street. When we crashed the car, Connie and I were on our way to Mexico. With the amount of money I had access to, we could have lived like a king and queen for the rest of our lives."

"What about the baby?" Jen asked.

"Once Connie found out she wouldn't be getting Billy's money, she panicked. She said she didn't want the brat in our lives, and she knew her parents would take care of him. I wanted to take my son with us, but she didn't want any part of it. She's one cold-hearted bitch."

The district attorney shook his head in dismay. "Will you be willing to testify against her at her trial?"

"Only if you take the death penalty off the table. I can handle life in prison, but I don't want to die. I also want her folks to send me pictures of Benjamin so I can keep up on him."

"You can consider the death penalty off the table. I can't guarantee how the boys grandparents will react to your request."

With Wade's statement recorded, typed up and signed, the meeting ended. Rhonda left the interrogation room more bewildered than ever. So far, she'd seen three sides of Connie. The belligerent one who could make a sailor blush with her language, the grieving widow who showed no emotion, and the sweet young thing who seduced Billy. Now a fourth side was appearing. Wade was right, she was a cold-hearted bitch.

"What will happen next?" she asked the district attorney.

"Wade will appear in court and admit everything to the judge. After that he will start serving his life sentence."

"How long before we can take Connie to trial?" Jen inquired.

"I'd like to say next week, but in reality, it won't be for at least three to four months. She should be convicted and starting to serve her sentence by her first wedding anniversary. My concerns are for her parents as well as her son. It would be much better if she confessed to everything and saved everyone involved the heartbreak of the trial. Unfortunately, she thinks she can win in court, which I doubt. The only good thing is that Wade has asked me to start the paperwork to sign over his inheritance to his son, with a portion of it to go to the Williams to help with the expense of raising him."

The events of the morning left Rhonda stunned. "What about the charges against him in Illinois?"

"We've been in contact with the DA out there and he's admitting to being part of hiding his mother's body. They've agreed to drop the charges since he will be serving a life sentence without the possibility of parole. It's worked out well for everyone involved."

"Everyone, except Benjamin. The poor kid. I hope upbringing trumps genes in his case."

Chapter Twenty-two

By the time Connie Riley went to trial, Jen and Paul were married. Rhonda and Mark were the matron of honor and the best man at the small wedding held in one of the wedding chapels on the strip. The other guests were Jen's father, as well as Paul's mother and sisters. Her father hosted a reception for their other friends at the casino where he worked. Since everyone there knew Jen, it was a lavish affair. Afterward, they left on a honeymoon to San Francisco.

The morning of the trial, Rhonda was pleased to see Jen waiting for her. "How was your honeymoon?" she asked before they entered the courtroom.

"It was wonderful. I've always wanted to go to San Francisco. We did lots of sightseeing as well as spending time together in the hotel room. I know nothing was a mystery since we've been living together for over a year. It was all different in a hotel room in a romantic city, though."

Once they entered the courtroom, Rhonda saw Bill's parents sitting behind the prosecution team while Connie's parents sat behind the defense table. As much as she wanted to reach out to each of them, she quietly took a seat in the center of the room where Mark, Paul, Karl and Tyson were seated.

"This is going to be a high-profile trial," Karl said, nodding toward the reporters sitting two rows behind them.

"I wish she would have taken a deal," Rhonda replied. "This has to be hard on the parents on both sides."

Before anyone could say anything more, Connie, with her defense team and the prosecution attorneys took their places at their respective tables. The prosecution portrayed Connie as little more than a black widow spider, having her husband killed and profiting from his death. On the other hand, the defense said she was nowhere near the scene of the murder and was completely innocent.

Included on the witness list for the prosecution were Wade Johnston, as well as Carlton Axton. They both portrayed her as the mastermind behind, not only the drugging of the candy Carlton delivered to the dressing room, but also the murder of her husband. Wade described, in detail, how Connie insisted he get her pregnant to get Billy to marry her.

Rhonda saw other band members in the gallery and wondered how they were taking this information about the people they worked with and trusted.

By the end of testimony for the first day, the prosecution rested their case. The witnesses for the defense wouldn't be heard until the next morning.

Rhonda was torn between her loyalties. Part of her wanted to be with Rick and Sue as well as the members of Bill's band. She also wanted to comfort Connie's parents. She knew they must be going through hell. From what she read in the tabloids; the press was portraying them as monsters for being the parents of someone like Connie.

It was Sue who made the decision much easier. After greeting Rhonda and Mark she went to where the Williams were standing. Rhonda was surprised when Mr. and Mrs. Williams joined their group.

"Everyone, you remember Pam and Jason Williams, Connie's parents. They're on the other side of this thing, but the press is giving them a bad reputation. I've invited them to come to dinner with us tonight."

Sue's generosity shocked Rhonda. It shouldn't have, since everyone seemed to embrace Pam and Jason.

"I can't thank any of you enough," Pam said. "We tried to talk to Connie and get her to plead guilty. She won't listen to us. After hearing what Wade and Carlton had to say today, I'm afraid she's going to get the death penalty. She has signed papers so we can adopt Benjamin and Bill's parents have been wonderful to us. Even though Benjamin isn't their grandson. They've reached out to us to take on a grandparent role in his life. In that, if in nothing else, we are blessed."

When they left the courthouse, Tyson said he'd arranged for a private dining room to accommodate the number of people who would be going to dinner with the two sides of the drama playing out at the courthouse.

After what had been a tension-filled day, they all needed the relaxation of a night without the worry about the situation they were faced with. They knew if any of them were alone, the negative thoughts would dominate their minds.

~ * ~

The next morning, Rhonda was surprised when the only witness called was Connie.

"I can't believe all the lies everyone is telling about me," she began. "I was certain Billy was my baby's father. I loved him and was devastated when he was murdered."

Her testimony went on and on until Rhonda was certain the jury could see through the lies the girl was spouting. By noon, the judge called for a recess.

After lunch, the district attorney began his cross-examination. "When you were arrested, you and Wade Johnston were heading to Mexico without your child. Why was that?"

"Wade was my rock. We've been friends ever since we were little kids."

"He's also your son's father. Was there a reason you didn't take the child with you?"

"Wade said the kid would slow us down. Thank goodness he wasn't with us when we had that accident. He might have been killed. We were going to send for him once we were settled."

"When did you know Wade was your son's father?"

"When the Riley's demanded a DNA test be done. When it came back saying Benjamin wasn't Billy's son, Wade had to be. He's the only other person I had sex with."

"If you were in love with Bill Riley, why would you have sexual relations with another man?"

"He wasn't another man. He was my friend with benefits."

"Were you using protection?"

"Billy always used a condom; I thought it might have broken or something. Wade didn't like to use a condom. But I knew all about the rhythm method. I was certain we were safe."

"Do you know what they call people who They're called parents. I think you know who the father of your child was, but the lure of Bill Riley's money was too enticing. You wanted his money not only for you but for your child. Did you even think he might want a DNA test after the baby was born? Is that why you wanted him killed?"

"Billy loved me," Connie sobbed. "He would have never questioned Benjamin being his. I'd give anything if Wade hadn't killed him. We would have been a family and..."

Loud sobs filled the courtroom, cutting off Connie's testimony. Not only was Connie crying, but so were both sets of parents.

The judge pounded his gavel and called for order. While Rick comforted Sue, Jason did the same for Pam.

Once order was restored, the DA returned to his original line of questioning. "Don't you think it's a strange coincidence that the will was registered, you were married, and your husband was killed within less than forty-eight hours?"

"It was what you called it, a strange coincidence. I-I loved Billy. We were going to be a happy family."

"A happy family with Bill raising someone else's child? How long did you think it would take before Bill divorced you once he knew the truth? Wasn't it that the only way you could get your hands on his money was to have him killed?"

Connie's face went completely white, and her eyes opened wide. Before she could answer, her lawyer got to his feet and yelled, "I object."

"Sustained," the judge ruled.

Rhonda knew what the DA was doing. By asking the question that wouldn't be answered, the jury would have the seed of doubt planted in their minds.

"I have nothing more for this witness," the DA said after the judge sustained the defense's objection.

By three in the afternoon, the closing arguments were made, and the jury was sent to the jury room for deliberation.

From past experiences, Rhonda knew it could be a long-drawn-out process. Still, she wasn't ready to leave the courthouse just in case the verdict came in early.

By five they were told the jury had been taken back to the hotel for the night and would begin deliberations again in the morning. Reluctantly, Rhonda, as well as several other people who were still hoping for an early verdict, left the courthouse.

~ * ~

The next morning, Rhonda returned to the courthouse. In the hallway, she saw Sue and Pam deep in conversation. Not wanting to interfere, she went in and took her seat.

Within minutes of her arrival, it was announced the jury sent a message saying they reached a unanimous decision. With the announcement, the tension seemed to be high, and the silence was deafening. Rhonda watched as the jury returned to the jury box.

"Madam Foreperson, have you reached a decision?" the judge asked.

"We have, Your Honor."

"On the charge of conspiracy to commit first degree murder, how do you find?"

"We find the defendant guilty."

Pam Williams screamed and collapsed into her husband's arms.

The judge banged his gavel. "Order in the courtroom," he demanded.

He turned his attention to Connie. "Connie Williams-Riley, you've been found guilty of conspiracy to commit the first-degree murder of your husband, William Riley. For now, you are remanded to the custody of the Clark County Sheriff's Office. We will convene again in two weeks for sentencing."

Rhonda watched as two matrons came forward to handcuff Connie and lead her away. She showed no emotions and didn't even turn toward her parents. Her reaction reminded Rhonda of the memorial service when she acted in the same way. Wade's description of her as a cold-hearted bitch suited her well.

"I don't know her anymore," Pam lamented.

"From everything we've heard over the last couple of days, I don't think we've known her since she took up with Wade and went out to Los Angeles. I think he has more to do with this than he told anyone, but we'll never know for certain. At least he's going to prison for the rest of his life," Jason consoled his wife. "It's a shame Benjamin will never know his parents, but maybe it's a blessing in disguise. She left him with us and made no move to contact us to check on him. If the Riley's hadn't found out Bill wasn't his father, I've been told she planned to take him to Wisconsin and never go back for him. He's better off with us."

Rhonda choked back her tears, not for Connie but for Pam and Jason. They had to be devastated at the thought they raised a monster.

As the DA walked out of the courtroom, Rhonda stopped him. "What can Connie expect to get for a sentence?"

"Why would you be concerned about what sentence she gets?"

"Not for the reason you might think. I'm worried about her parents as well as her son. I'd hate to think of her coming back into their lives anytime in the future."

"I expect the judge will give her at least sixty years. There will be periodic hearings for parole, but giving the circumstances of this crime, I doubt she could be looking at parole anytime in the future."

"Sixty years?" Pam questioned from behind Rhonda. "That means I'll never see her free again. Maybe it is for the best. I can't imagine what kind of an influence she would be on Benjamin."

For the first time, Rhonda wondered where the baby was during the trial. "Speaking of Benjamin, where is he?"

"We brought him out with us. My sister and her husband are retired and lived in Mesquite. We've been staying with them, and they've been watching him during the day while we've been here."

"Will you be here for the sentencing?"

Jason shook his head, a look of dismay on his face. "I need to go back to work, but Pam and Benjamin will stay until this whole mess is over. After that, we will be going back to Illinois and try to forget any of this happened."

~ * ~

Two weeks later, Rhonda and Jen were back in the courtroom to witness the sentencing of Connie Williams-Riley.

Rick and Sue were also in the courtroom, along with Pam. It was amazing to see the two women holding each other's hand in consolation. Also in attendance was Bill's best friend, Rusty.

"Before I impose the sentence, I will entertain any statements from those who were closest to not only Connie, but also Bill."

Rusty was the first to get to his feet. "Bill Riley was and always will be my best friend. We were also business partners for the past several years. I grieve his senseless murder and the loss of his talent to the world. I am sorry we ever met you, Connie. I have never known anyone who was so greedy that they would mastermind a murder to get their hands on his money. Bill would have given you anything you ever wanted. He was blind to what you were because he loved you. I hope you have many years to consider your crime and beg for forgiveness."

The next to speak was Rick Riley. "You took more than you will ever know from my wife and myself. Bill was our only surviving child. For a while, we thought your son was our grandson. You were cruel enough to take away our son, but you also denied us the only grandchild we will ever have. Thank God your parents are better people than you will ever be. They are allowing us to act as grandparents to Benjamin, although it will never be the same as it would have been if he was Bill's child. I pray you will never walk free again and when you die, may God have mercy on your soul."

Pam merely shook her head when asked if she wanted to make a statement. Rhonda understood, there were no words for her to speak that would ever express the thoughts she had about her daughter.

"If these are the last of the statements, do you have anything to say for yourself before I pass sentence?"

Connie got to her feet, turning to look at her mother for what might be the last time. "I know you adopted Benjamin. Please let him know I was his mother. I know what I did was wrong, but…" For the first time Connie broke down and cried. "I have nothing more to say."

"Then I sentence you to sixty years to life in the state prison for women. You will first be eligible for parole in 2056."

With no other parting words, Connie allowed the matron to lead her out of the courtroom.

"Will you and Jason be all right?" Jen asked Pam.

"Thank you for your concern, but Rick and Sue said they would help us with Benjamin. They've also set aside a trust fund from some of the money from Bill's estate. Besides that, Wade has signed over all his inheritance money, which is a considerable amount. We've already invested the money, with a minimal amount to be sent to us for his needs. We will be able to draw that from the interest and not touch the principle."

Rhonda knew Benjamin would be raised with love. She only hoped love would overcome the blood and genes flowing through his veins.

Epilogue
Six months after Connie's trial and sentencing

Mark and Rhonda were enjoying a quiet evening at home when the words *Special Bulletin* interrupted the program they were watching.

The reporter was standing outside of the penitentiary. "In a strange twist to the Billy Roller murder case, Wade Johnston, confessed killer of Billy Roller, was killed today while taking a shower. The inmate who killed him with a home-made shiv, has been apprehended and is in solitary confinement."

The man paused, giving Rhonda and Mark a chance to exchange shocked glances.

"In other news, Connie Williams-Riley is serving her sentence at the women's prison. When asked about Wade's death, she showed no emotion whatsoever. Within the next hour, she suffered a brain aneurysm. She is listed in critical condition in the facility's infirmary."

"Interesting," Mark said, once the program they were watching resumed. "I certainly didn't want anything so drastic to happen to either one of them, but maybe it's a blessing in disguise. At least Jason and Pam won't ever have to worry about either of them coming to take Benjamin away from them. They will also be able to file for Social Security from both parents."

"If they're smart, they won't try to get it."

"Why do you say that?"

"I have a feeling neither of them ever worked an honest job in their lives. Wade was born with a silver spoon in his mouth and once his father died, he was independently wealthy. As for Connie, she probably did a lot of babysitting, but I doubt she ever had an actual job. That said, I doubt either of them would be eligible for Social Security benefits. Besides, I doubt Pam and Jason will need it. The amount of money Wade put in their name will be enough to support Benjamin for the rest of his life."

Mark nodded in agreement. "Now that you have this case completely put to bed, let's change the subject. How would you feel about planning a vacation?"

"That sounds wonderful. Where are you thinking of taking me?"

"I thought you would look damn good in a bikini, laying on the beach in Jamaica for about a week. I stopped at the travel agency today and picked up some literature on an all-inclusive resort in Ocho Rios."

Rhonda looked at the brochure Mark retrieved from its hiding place between the couch cushions. "When do you think we could go?"

"I checked the school calendar, and it looks like I can get away over the Thanksgiving holiday. Since I'm not involved in football, it will be perfect. I asked and we can book a vacation where we will be spending Thanksgiving in Jamaica. Do you think you can get the time off?"

"This far in advance, I think it can be arranged. I can hardly wait to start shopping for a wardrobe to take with me."

"I figured that's what you'd say, so I made a tentative reservation. We should have the best Thanksgiving ever this year."

Also by the Author
at
Rogue Phoenix Press

Man in the Lake
Rhonda Pohs Mysteries Book 1

Rhonda Pohs has been hired as a token woman on a small town police force. Other than traffic stops on the highway, her only other duties are to meet with families after a loved one has been killed in a traffic accident. A call from a distraught wife about her missing husband comes in just before one of a man floating in a local lake. Chief Franks send Rhonda to check on one of the most cheating husbands in town. While Rhonda is talking to Kitty Reedman, she is informed that the man floating in the lake is Karl Reedman, Kitty's husband. From the get go, Rhonda is embroiled in solving the mystery of Karl's murder at the risk of her life.

Murder in the Meadow
Rhonda Pohs Mysteries Book 2

As Rhonda moves to a detective position with the county sheriff's office her first lead case is the murder of the most hated man in the county. George Atkins has been killed with his own pitchfork while spreading manure. The fact the elderly man was out in a raging blizzard makes no sense. Why would he be out in such inclement weather? As the case progresses, threats are made against other members in the family, until Rhonda finally reveals the most unexpected suspect with a deep seeded hatred for the Atkins family for what he believes has been done to him in the past.

Murder by Mistake
Rhonda Pohs Mysteries Book 3

Dressed as Bonnie and Clyde, Rhonda and her husband are on their way to a Halloween party, when they witness a drive by shooting. The man who is shot is John Richardson, who is handing out candy dressed up as a scarecrow with a jack-o-lantern covering his face. Going into detective mode, completely unaware of how she is dressed, she calls in the crime and rushes to the scene. To her dismay, she soon learns John is in the hospital and his grandson, Sean, has taken his place. Joined by her partner, Phil, Rhonda must decide if the intended victim is John or his beloved grandson. No matter which one it is, why would anyone want to take either of their lives?

Reunion for Murder
Rhonda Pohs Mysteries Book 4

When Rhonda is called to a private residence to investigate a murder, she finds this is the site of the twenty-fifth-class reunion for her former partner, Phil. With her new partner, Martin, she is forced to question all the classmates regarding the murder of Pete Potter, even Phil. Pete has been found floating in a small lake on the property. The owner of a local insurance agency it's hard telling who would want him dead. When it's revealed he's a transvestite, the suspect pool widens. Could it be someone from the community he embraced in Madison, or someone closer to home? The odds are 50/50 in each direction, so Rhonda must decide which way to look.

Murder in Red Rock Canyon
Rhonda Pohs Mysteries Book 5

Following her husband when he takes a new position, Rhonda leaves

Wisconsin behind to begin a new life in Las Vegas, Nevada. Without a job for the first time, she is thrilled when she obtains a position with the Clark County Sheriff's department. To celebrate her new job, she and her husband, Mark, go to Red Rock Canyon for a relaxing day of sightseeing. Even before she is scheduled to begin her job, she finds herself at the center of a murder. The victim, a college student, has been killed close to the petroglyphs using an ancient Native American weapon,. Have the ancients returned to protect their history or is there a modern-day predator trying to confuse her with the use of ancient weapons?

About the Author

Wife, mother, grandmother and great grandmother, Sherry is first and foremost an author. She and her husband of sixty years enjoy their retirement and wonder how they ever had time to work. Sherry calls her husband a saint for putting up with an author.

VISIT OUR WEBSITE
FOR THE FULL INVENTORY
OF QUALITY BOOKS:

http://www.roguephoenixpress.com

Rogue Phoenix Press
Representing Excellence in Publishing

Quality trade paperbacks and downloads
in multiple formats,
in genres ranging from historical to contemporary romance,
mystery and science fiction.
Visit the website then bookmark it.

www.ingramcontent.com/pod-product-compliance
Lightning Source LLC
Chambersburg PA
CBHW070325130626
46556CB00007B/2735